Praise

"Lee Driver has w~~ ~~~~ ~~~~ ~~ has excellent plotting, brilliant characterizations and an enthralling storyline."
— *Midwest Book Review*

"Lee Driver's Chase Dagger/Sara Morningsky series is one of the few truly dependable mystery series being published today. You always know what to expect with Driver: the unexpected."
— Craig Clarke, Top 1000 Reviewer

"The appeal of cross-genre novels is sometimes difficult to target, but this one should have no trouble attracting readers from either the mystery or the fantasy side of the fence." — *Booklist*

"In Driver's novels it is impossible to separate the lure of the plot and the magnetism of the characters. The chance to catch a hell of a mystery and the growing, unfolding enigma of such characters as these is exceedingly rare. Don't miss the opportunity."
— Lisa DuMond, www.sfsite.com

This is a delightfully nontraditional mystery that should appeal to a wide variety of readers. Let the series continue. — *Booklist*

The attendant breezy sex, violence, and action, coupled with bits of Indian lore and Einstein the talking macaw, should have readers clamoring for the projected next novel. — *Library Journal*

Also by Lee Driver

Chase Dagger Series

Fatal Storm
Chasing Ghosts
The Unseen
Full Moon-Bloody Moon
The Good Die Twice

Short Stories

Sara Morningsky, *Mystery in Mind Anthology*
The Thirteenth Hole, *Mystery in Mind Anthology*

Written as S.D. Tooley

Sam Casey Series

Destiny Kills
What Lies Within
Echoes from the Grave
Restless Spirit
Nothing Else Matters
When the Dead Speak

Short Stories

Mysteries to Die For, a short story collection in the Kindle store

For Middle School/Young Adult Readers

Remy and Roadkill Series

The Skull

> Some of the above titles are also available in large print, audio and eBook formats

The Vaporizer

Lee Driver

Full Moon Publishing

This book is a work of fiction. Names, characters, places and incidents are the product of the author's imagination or are used fictitiously. Any resemblance to actual events, locales or persons, living or dead, is coincidental. Any slights of people, places, or organizations is purely unintentional.

Copyright ©2013   by Lee Driver
All rights reserved.
This book, or parts thereof, may not be reproduced in any form without permission.

Library of Congress Control Number: 2013930585

ISBN 978-0-9888683-1-1

Published March 2013

Printed in the United States of America

Full Moon Publishing LLC
433 Mystic Point Drive
Bluffton, SC 29909

www.fullmoonpub.com

THE VAPORIZER

1

She was the first to awaken. The air was thick with the scent of sweat, mold, and dirt. Several times she had stirred, but drifted off to sleep again. This time she was determined to stay awake. Her eyelids fluttered. She lay still for several minutes wondering why her entire body felt leaden, the muscles shaky. For a moment the darkness and earth scents made her wonder if she had fallen asleep in the forest. She searched for a canopy of trees and flickering of stars in the sky. Nothing. Only darkness.

One deep breath, then another. One eyelid, then two. Another deep breath. Just when she tried to shift, to get the blood flowing in her limbs, she became aware of a heavy weight on her right side and someone's breath in her hair. The weight shifted and someone moaned softly. She froze, trying to remember where she had been. Her bedroom or someone else's? She certainly wouldn't have gone home with a stranger. What time was it? What day? The weight shifted again, a portion of it, possibly an arm, raised. She heard a scratching sound, like sandpaper, then detected the scent of a woodsy aftershave.

"Dagger?" she whispered.

"Huh? What the…" There was a thud and a painful, "Ow!" The weight shifted again. "Sara?"

"Where are we?" She called on her enhanced sight, the eyes of the hawk, and surveyed their surroundings. "I can't see anything." And she couldn't, other than the heat radiating off of Dagger's body. She struggled to free herself from his weight.

"I think we're in the trunk of a car," Dagger said. "It must be a shit can electric car because this trunk can barely fit the two of us." He tried to free his left arm, but it was trapped under Sara's head. "What the hell happened? I don't remember a damn thing."

"I don't either, and my head is killing me. Did we go out drinking?"

Dagger remained silent for several seconds, his mind trying to conjure up a timeline while tiny pricks of fear worked their way up his spine. He tasted something strange in his mouth. "I think we were drugged." Dagger made another startling discovery…the lack of fabric against his skin or Sara's. "Uh, and I think someone took our clothes."

"Naked?" Sara rubbed the fingers of her left hand against her thigh and felt skin. She wiggled her toes and realized even her shoes had been removed. Dagger was right. "How did this happen?" She groaned. The effort to talk made her head spin. "I don't think there's much oxygen in here." Sara felt around the roof of the car trunk. "Aren't there safety latches in cars these days?" Dagger's weight pressed against her right side, trapping her arm, and something pulsated against her thigh. "Could you move your hand off my leg?"

"Uhhh, that's not my hand, but thanks for the compliment."

"Ewwww." Sara shoved hard. She heard another thud as Dagger's head slammed against the wall.

"Ow. Hey, there's only so much room in here."

"Shouldn't you ask a girl to dinner first?"

"I'm a guy. Satin sheets, flesh pressed against flesh, and…" He inhaled long and deep, feeling that third hand getting harder. "Damn, you smell good."

"Wait." Sara's fingers scratched the fabric beneath her. "Satin sheets? Is there a satin pillow under my head?"

He felt his way around Sara's shoulder toward her neck and touched a satiny mound of fabric. Satin sheets, satin pillow, tight enclosure. "Damn. I think we're in a coffin."

2

"Let's just calm down and think for a minute." Dagger tried to shift his weight, but the side of the coffin pressed against his back. "We weren't with Simon last night, were we?"

"Simon? What does he have to do with anything?"

How like Sara not to realize all the sexual innuendos Simon never failed to inject into any conversation. "My pendant!" In such a tight space, he couldn't lift either hand to confirm the presence of his leather cord necklace.

Sara called upon the enhanced eyesight of the hawk to enable her to see in the dark. "It's still there."

"I don't like this. I can't remember a damn thing. I don't even know what day it is."

"I can't either," Sara had to admit. "I think you're right. Someone drugged us."

Dagger pressed one hand against the lid and shoved. The lid wouldn't budge.

"Why don't you try pressing your back against it?" Sara suggested.

Dagger suppressed a smile. "To do that I'm going to have to lie on top of you. So don't panic if my third hand has a mind of its own."

"Did I ever tell you that my grandfather taught me how to kill a chicken by wringing its neck?"

Dagger waffled between the thought of Sara's fingers around his third hand and the pain of being wrung like a chicken. "Wait. We have no way of knowing if this coffin is buried under six feet of dirt. Opening the lid might not be a good idea. Do you smell any dirt?"

"Yes. It isn't overwhelming so I doubt we are under six feet of it." Sara called upon the enhanced ability of the gray wolf to detect the outside atmosphere. "Dirt, mold, dampness. I don't think the coffin is buried." Her left hand reached over Dagger's body and found a one-inch gap between the lid and the top ridge of the coffin. "Someone obviously didn't want us to suffocate. He propped one side open."

"How thoughtful. Remind me to thank him before I shoot him in the head." Dagger shifted and cautiously rolled on top of Sara. "Here goes." This was so not a good idea. Working and living platonically with his partner was one thing, but this skin-to-skin contact did not bode well for his self control. He tried not to think of how one good thrust and he would be where no man had been before.

Sara slapped his side. "Did you just moan?"

Did I? "No. I thought that was you."

Sara slapped him again. Dagger raised up, his back pressed against the satin lining of the lid. The coffin folded open on its hinge. More darkness greeted him. He raised the lid all the way and straightened. Sara slid out from under him and sat up.

"See anything?" Dagger said. A slice of dim light broke through a small pane of glass in a door. Other than that one glimmer, he couldn't see a damn thing. Sara, on the other hand, had talents valuable to his business. Sara could shift into a hawk or a wolf. Even in her human form she could call upon the eyesight of the hawk or senses of the wolf.

She saw coffins stacked against three sides of the stone structure. Brass nameplates stated the names of the deceased. "I think we're in a crypt or mausoleum."

Dagger carefully climbed out of the coffin. "See our clothes anywhere?"

Sara scanned the concrete floor littered with insect carcasses, the coffins covered with years of dust and grime. Then she caught sight of Dagger's naked body. "Wow." She hadn't realized she had said it out loud.

"Wow what?" Dagger could barely make out Sara's image in the shadows. He felt his wrist. His watch was still there.

"I don't see our clothes. I don't even remember if I had a purse with me. What about your wallet? Your identification? Car keys?"

"If someone took my gun, I'll kill him." Dagger pressed a button on his watch. "I criticized Skizzy for making this space cadet watch, but it has proven useful more than once." The watch served as a telephone and also a tracking device.

"Yo. Skizzy at your service. Who did you kill today?"

Dagger could imagine his friend sitting in his bunker surrounded by multiple computer monitors. For such a small phone, Skizzy's voice couldn't have been any clearer if he had been standing in the same room.

"Just tell me where the hell I'm at." He could hear the wheels of a chair rolling across a concrete floor, then fingers tapping on a keyboard. Behind him he heard cloth being torn.

"Portland Cemetery in LaPorte. What the hell are you doing in a cemetery? They built that place on the farm where that loony lady lured husbands to be, killed them and fed their remains to her pigs."

"That's a pleasant thought. Just come get us and bring some clothes."

A Hummer pulled to a stop at the edge of the gravel road.

Dawn crept through the trees while a ghostly mist slithered along the cemetery floor. Two figures slammed out of the vehicle and advanced toward the crypt.

Sara and Dagger emerged from the crypt. Sara wrapped the coffin's satin lining tightly around her body. Dagger had a heart-shaped satin pillow pressed in front of his groin area. He would have felt the chill in the air had he not been so overheated from the coffin. He sought refuge behind a shrub which barely clung to the remains of its leaves.

"Why the hell did you bring him?" Dagger yelled at the scarecrow of a man while motioning to a portly black man who's grin practically split his face in half.

"Simon had extra clothes," Skizzy said. "Mine could fit Sara, but they certainly wouldn't fit you." He looked as though he had been roused from sleep as stray gray hairs wrestled free from his ponytail. His wrinkled camouflage shirt and pants hung on his bony frame.

Simon's dark eyes danced and he did little to hide his amusement. He had a rolling gait as his spindly legs struggled to hold up his rotund body. "In a coffin. Naked." Simon chuckled as Dagger pressed the pillow tighter against his body. "That musta been hard."

"Was it ever," Sara whispered, then realized her words carried in the still air. She felt her face flush as Simon and Skizzy both barked out a laugh. She could see Dagger struggle to suppress a smile.

"Oh I bet Mister Happy stood up straight and tall, looking around, sniffing the air." Skizzy's eyebrows did a little dance.

"Will you just fuckin' hand me some clothes?" Dagger growled.

"Wait." Skizzy pulled out a hand-held object that looked like a wand. "Can never be too careful. Never know if aliens abducted you and implanted something or did some weird sex experiments on you."

"Shit. I didn't even consider BettaTec," Dagger said as Skizzy ran the wand up one side of his body and down the other. BettaTec was a covert organization Dagger used to work for. When Skizzy wanded him the first time, he had discovered that a microchip had been implanted in the back of his neck. The cord necklace Sara's grandmother had given him contained copper wire which prevented electronic detection.

Somehow, as only women can do, Sara had managed to tie the sheet in such a way to allow her to slip into the pants and shirt Skizzy had brought without exposing herself.

"Looks like you're clean. Now we gotta check girlie."

Once presentable, Sara took the sheet and wrapped it around Dagger. Simon handed him a pair of women's silk underpants that looked large enough for two of him to fit in.

"You brought me Eunie's underwear?" Dagger could feel his hands balling into fists. "I swear, if you are responsible for us ending up naked in a coffin together, I will beat you to a pulp. Hand me the pants."

"You're going commando?" Simon tossed him a pair of his slacks. He held a belt he knew Dagger would need since Simon had been growing his gut for years. Dagger grumbled as he cinched the belt and glared at how the slacks barely reached his ankles.

"I wanted to bring one of Eunie's leopard-skin printed slacks. I'm sure those would have fit you better."

"You know what you could have done with those slacks. And if you brought a silk blouse for me to wear I will fuckin' shoot you where you stand."

"Wow, testy." Simon handed him a navy blue postal worker's shirt.

Dagger slipped into the shirt and buttoned it. His hair

hung loose past the collar. If it had been in a ponytail, he wasn't about ready to search the coffin for the missing band.

"It was scary," Sara said. "We could have been buried under six feet of dirt." She looked back at the cold gray crypt. The mist was drifting closer as though summoned by the cemetery occupants. "Should we dust for fingerprints to find out who did this to us?"

"No. I just want to get home and try to piece together the past twenty-four hours." Dagger paused and looked at his friends. "What day is it?"

"Saturday," Simon said. "I delivered mail on Thursday. That's the last time I saw you." Although Dagger had a postal box, Simon preferred to deliver their mail to Sara's home on the outskirts of Cedar Point, Indiana, a town of over one hundred thousand which hugged the shores of Lake Michigan.

"I haven't seen or talked to you since last Tuesday," Skizzy added.

"Were we working a case? Headed out of town? What the hell happened?" Dagger patted his hip out of habit. "Where's my Kimber?" His Kimber .45 was his baby. He never left home without it.

Simon ushered them to the Hummer like a mother hen. "Let's get you back home and figure out if all of your vehicles are there. Then Skizzy can track whichever one is missing. Do you need to get some sleep first?"

"Hell, for all we know we've been sleeping for the past day and a half." Dagger looked down at his bare feet and the slacks which hit mid-calf and growled another obscenity.

3

"Food." Sara grabbed a piece of bacon and shoved it in her mouth. "I'm famished."

"Got a bottle of aspirin on the table, too," Simon said. He held a spatula in one hand and wore a dish towel tucked in his waist like an apron. Skizzy had dropped off the three of them at Sara's house and went back to his bunker beneath the pawn shop to start to search for his missing vehicle.

"Felt good to take a shower and wash the cobwebs out of my hair." Sara raked her fingers through her waist-length hair. The sun's rays revealed a myriad of shades from blonde to the darkest of browns.

"Feels even better to wear my own clothes." Dagger walked in dressed in his basic black cargo pants and shirt. A check of his garage revealed that his vehicles and Sara's PT Cruiser were accounted for. However, when Skizzy checked his stable of cars, he discovered his 1962 baby blue Cadillac Coupe de Ville missing. Although Dagger didn't remember taking it, Skizzy had in the past told Dagger to help himself if he ever needed a vehicle that didn't have a registered plate or a vehicle I.D. number. And Skizzy didn't remember the last time he had checked his garage.

"Did Skizzy drop off the urine samples at the clinic?" Dagger poured himself a cup of coffee and sat down at the granite table. He shook out two aspirins from the bottle and washed them down with a sip of coffee.

"Yep. Handed his guy a Benjamin and asked him to put a rush on the tests." Simon opened the oven and checked on his potato and cheese frittata while Sara pulled out a bowl of fruit and pitcher of orange juice from the fridge.

Once they filled their plates and sat down, Simon asked, "Find any notes on your desk to give you a clue?"

"Nothing. I checked the garbage can by the desk and the ones in my bedroom and in the kitchen. Usually I place active case folders right on my desk."

"If they aren't buried under junk," Sara added under her breath, avoiding Dagger's glare.

"What about license, charge cards, money?" Simon grabbed the carafe and refilled his coffee cup.

"Everything gone, even my Kimber. That gun cost me over a thousand dollars."

Simon turned to Sara. "What about your identification?"

"I am missing my cream colored purse, and I didn't see my wallet or even my Kel-Tec anywhere in the house."

Simon ran a hand across his face. His hair may be gray and he may look like a toddling old man ready to retire from the post office, but he was also a former Viet Nam sniper and someone Dagger trusted to have his back.

"Hmmmm." Simon contemplated a subject that made him smile. "You two didn't go to a justice of the peace, did you?"

Sara felt a rush of heat as both she and Dagger stole a glance at the ring fingers on their left hands. "Receipts." She jumped from the table and grabbed sales receipts from the counter. "I did the grocery shopping Thursday."

"Do you have something constructive to suggest, old man?"

"I'm just saying, people have gotten drunk and done outrageous things before." Simon enjoyed making Dagger uncomfortable. Both he and Eunie felt the two were destined for each other, even though Dagger preferred to live life unencumbered, to fly solo and be free to pick up and move on at a moment's notice. He had had many opportunities in the past to leave, to keep on the run. Then he met Sara and for some reason he convinced himself that staying in one place would be safer.

"Here's something constructive I can offer. Why don't you ask your receptionist."

"Einstein," Sara and Dagger blurted in unison.

Sara held up a bowl of fresh fruit. "Look Einstein. Food."

Dagger inspected the food bowls of nuts, fruit and vegetables sitting around the aviary. His macaw hadn't been left alone for too long.

A blur of scarlet and blue peeked out from between the fronds of a tall tree in the corner of the aviary. Although artificial, the tree reached fifteen feet in height. Lush green outdoor carpeting added a natural feel to the twelve hundred square foot room.

Einstein had a photographic memory so if he had overheard Sara and Dagger talking about their plans, he might know what case they had been working and where they had been headed to last. However, Einstein didn't look happy to have been left alone without any warning.

"Bad people hurt us, Einstein," Sara tried to explain. She had a habit of babying the macaw whereas Dagger played the bad cop to her good cop.

Dagger shoved his hands on his hips and glared at the macaw. "Last phone call, Einstein. Now."

"AWWKKK, DAGGER INVESTIGATIONS. YOU GRAB UM, WE'LL SLAB UM. AWWKKK."

"Einstein." Dagger heaved out a sigh in frustration. "Did I make any calls?"

The macaw let out a loud whistle which made Simon cover his ears. "You really have him trained," Simon said. "You may have to get yourself another receptionist."

A sound like bubbles popping in rhythm exploded from Dagger's computer. He slid the soundproof door to the aviary closed and the three of them assembled around the desk.

"What's up?"

Skizzy's smiling face showed up on the monitor. "Found my sixty-two Cadillac. Tracked it to a parking lot outside of a vacant strip mall on Calhoun."

"Give me the address. I'll go pick it up."

"No can do. Just heard on the police scanner that they found a body in the trunk. Looks like you two were busy last night."

"Shit," Dagger hissed under his breath. "Have they I.D.'d the guy?"

"Just that he's young, Hispanic, possibly a gang member. Oh, and it appears everyone's favorite cop is working the case."

"Is there anything on that car that can link it to you, Skizzy?" Simon asked.

"Nope. Course that isn't saying there ain't something inside the car that links it to Dagger and Sara."

Neither Dagger nor Simon noticed that Sara had retreated upstairs to her bedroom.

4

Sergeant Padre Martinez watched as one of the techs used a portable fingerprint monitor to take the prints of the deceased. He stood in a rumpled trench coat next to a wiry black man who carefully examined the body on the gurney. Luther Jamison, Cedar Point's chief medical examiner, appeared far younger than his actual years. Padre, on the other hand, calculated his aging by the number of gray hairs left on his head. This job was going to kill him.

"No blood in the trunk," the disheveled detective said. He mutilated a piece of gum as he spoke. He stepped closer to the passenger side door as a female tech used tweezers to hold up a long strand of dark hair. "I doubt that long hair came from our deceased, Ellen."

"How astute, Padre." The crime tech coaxed the strand into a clear plastic bag.

A strange four-legged animal crept behind a row of hedges. It was strange in the sense that its coat wasn't the typical hues of a gray wolf. The fur had various shades as dark as the blackest brown to mahogany and as light as ash. And wolves didn't have eyes the color of Caribbean waters. Pups were born with blue eyes, but the color changed to yellow, brown or green as they matured.

The gray wolf watched with cunning intellect. Its ears

perked when it heard the detective, as though it understood about hair and forensic evidence. The turquoise eyes followed the woman's movements as she zipped the evidence bag shut and handed it to the crumpled detective who held it up and examined the contents.

The wolf calculated the number of men and women searching the area for more evidence. It was aware of the number of people on the scene who carried weapons, and calculated the distance from where it hid to the location of the crime scene van.

The back of the van yawned open. A young tech, whom the detective had called a newbie, methodically logged in the various evidence bags. The wolf slowly stood, then moved to an opening between the hedges, a direct line to the crime scene van. And it waited.

Padre gave one last inspection of the vehicle's trunk. "Let's tow this baby in and go over it with a fine tooth comb." He walked over to the gurney to find the medical examiner rolling the body onto its side.

"I don't see any blood on him, no visible wounds." Luther gently grabbed one arm and turned it over. He did the same with the other arm. "No track marks. No bruises. Maybe I'll find out more when I get him back on my slab."

The detective scanned the surrounding area. The boarded up motel at the tail end of a strip mall had given up its struggle to survive. Very few customers frequented this part of town except for the sale days for the grocery store across the street. The strip mall resembled a turnstile with businesses coming and going so frequently the business signs were barely hung before they had to be removed. What a perfect place to dump a body. If it hadn't been for a curious bystander (translation:

would-be car thief), the police would have never discovered the body.

Detective Martinez gave a slight nod of his head toward the tech snapping photos. The camera made a smooth movement from the car's trunk to the small crowd of onlookers. Hopefully, they might find a face in the crowd, someone a little more curious than the others, someone with a slight indication of triumph and satisfaction.

"When do you think you'll be ready to cut this puppy open?" Padre asked.

Luther scratched the short bristle of graying hair clinging to his scalp. Dark eyes regarded the deceased through wire-rimmed glasses. "Got a few in front of him. With any luck, later today. If not, first thing tomorrow morning. I'll give you a call."

From the opposite end of the parking lot a city tow truck slowly backed up toward the Cadillac. Its incessant beeping echoed off the decaying building. The techs and police officers moved aside as did most of the bystanders. Nothing more to see. The wolf kept its eyes on the zip lock bag resting on the back bed of the van. Just as the tech lifted the evidence bag with the strand of hair and while everyone's eyes focused on the tow truck, the wolf made its move. It charged toward the van, leaped at the man, snatched the bag from his fingertips, and tore off for the woods in back of the motel.

It paid little attention to the yells from the officers and laughs from the onlookers. It had to reach cover before anyone started shooting. It stayed off of worn footpaths and wove its way between bushes and thorny underbrush, feeling the spikes tearing at its fur and hearing the tramping of feet chasing after it.

A dip toward a creek gave it the cover needed. It leaped toward an overhanging limb. Its paws quickly changed into talons as it took a firm hold on the limb. The evidence bag, which had once been tightly held between the wolf's teeth, now nestled tightly in the beak of a gray hawk. It crisscrossed several limbs as it climbed higher. Then it took flight, its powerful wing beats leading it away from the forest, away from the crime scene.

5

Masculine but bland. How else could anyone describe Dagger's taste in décor? His was the larger of the two bedrooms and Sara kept quiet about the gray and black hues he had chosen for the furnishings. He rarely bothered making the bed, claiming it would only get messed again. Sara had learned the hard way to just close the bedroom door on the rare occasions they had company.

Various pieces of gym equipment claimed the left side of Dagger's bedroom. The thermostat on the wall hid a keypad which opened a vault door cleverly concealed in the wall of mirrors.

Sara found Dagger standing in front of a monitor which displayed a world map. Two red lights blinked as they circled the globe, one in the upper hemisphere, the second in the lower hemisphere. One stationary blue light represented Cedar Point.

"Have they moved?" Sara stood next to him, the plastic evidence bag in her hand.

"No, fortunately."

"Face it, Dagger. If BettaTec had kidnapped us, I doubt we would still be in Cedar Point. They would have carted us off, or at least you, to one of their facilities. Or killed us," she added under her breath.

"Did you check your closet?" Dagger had suggested Sara check to see if any of her clothes were missing which could give them a hint where they were Friday night.

"I'm missing my cream-colored crop pants and my new boots which I'm really upset about. They cost me one hundred dollars." Sara didn't start to shop until after she met Dagger. Her grandmother had made all of her clothes. Once she discovered shopping malls and catalogs, she started to see how other women dressed.

Sara had been raised on a reservation in Montana. After her parents died in a house fire, her grandparents moved her for fear people would discover Sara's shapeshifting abilities. When her grandparents moved to the three hundred acres in Cedar Point, Sara rarely left the safety and security of their property, so fearful of strangers and the outside world. It was her grandmother who believed Sara's talents could be useful.

At that time Dagger's office had been in an apartment above a bar. Too small of a space for a loud and rowdy macaw. After Sara's grandmother passed away, Dagger offered Sara a job and moved into the converted automobile showroom which had been her grandparent's house. Theirs was a working relationship. He paid rent for his living and working space, and the dealer service area worked well as an aviary for Einstein. He also paid her a nice salary as his assistant.

"What about you?" Sara asked. "Silly question," she quickly added. Everything Dagger owned was either black or gray, and he had never counted how many black cargo pants he owned.

"I do know all of my sportcoats are there and my suits so we didn't go anywhere formal."

Sara noticed a piece of paper with numbers on it sitting on the desk below the world map. "What are these?"

Dagger gave a shrug. "Numbers I've been seeing in my sleep. Thought I'd see if they were coordinates, but they aren't." He folded the paper and shoved it in his pocket. "Must mean something, just haven't figured out what." Dagger saw the evidence bag in her hand and pulled it from her grasp. "Did you forget the rule about shifting during the daylight?"

"I was careful."

"Sara." He bit back the harsh criticism. He braced his arms against the desk, his muscles quivering from the anger building. It was a challenge not to shake some sense into her. "There are cameras these days. If they aren't on buildings or at traffic lights, then people are always pointing their cell phones at anything they think would garner attention on *YouTube*."

"I was careful," she repeated.

He turned away from the dresser, away from the clear plastic bag with that one strand of hair. "Careful doesn't cut it." He realized by the tremble of her bottom lip that he had crossed the line. "I can't deal with this right now. Simon's downstairs and could overhear."

They found Simon by the aviary coaxing Einstein with a cheese curl. The scarlet macaw turned one yellow-ringed eye toward the postman, then looked at the cheese curl. "Come on, Einstein. These are your favorites."

"Making yourself useful?" Dagger said.

"Hey, I made you breakfast, cleaned up the kitchen. Now I'm just waiting for a ride home. I can always call Eunie if you're too busy. She's back from her fun weekend with her old college friends."

Dagger handed Simon the slacks and shirt he had borrowed, then took the cheese curl from him. "We can leave now. Maybe if I drive around town something might spark a memory." He held up the cheese curl just outside of Einstein's reach. "What have you got to say for yourself, Einstein?"

The macaw eyed the treat. "CHARGE IT!" He snatched the cheese curl from Dagger's fingers and flew to the tree.

"Credit card," Sara and Dagger said in unison.

"What does that mean?" Simon followed them to Dagger's desk.

"It means the charges on my credit card could tell me where I've been." Dagger pounded out his sign on and password for his account. He clicked on his current statement and checked the last few entries. "Huh."

"Huh, what?" Simon leaned closer, then he started to chuckle. "The Ritz Hotel. Wonder what you two could have been doing there."

"For six hundred and eighty five dollars it was either a very good meal…" Dagger started.

Simon chuckled, long and deep. "Or a very nice room."

6

The Ritz Hotel hosted a number of conventions for corporations that wanted something on a smaller scale than offered by Chicago hotels. Elegant and pricey, its close proximity to a variety of casinos made it a favorite of tourists.

They crossed glistening marble floors to the reception desk. Glass tube elevators were numerous and carried visitors up to all twelve floors. The suites on the twelfth floor lined the north side of the hotel providing a fantastic view of Lake Michigan.

Sara tried not to gawk like a tourist at the lavish furnishings. "I certainly don't remember being here recently," she whispered. "This is a hotel I could see Sheila in." Dagger didn't reply which told her he probably made a few visits with Sheila when they dated.

"Welcome to the Ritz. I'm Donna. How may I help you?" Spit-shined and polished without a hair out of place, the young woman looked as prim and proper as a parochial school teacher in her neatly pressed uniform blouse.

Dagger had to punt because, like Sara, he didn't recall being there recently. He laid his credit card statement on the counter. "Can you tell me about these charges?" There were two charges on his statement, one for over two hundred dollars and another for close to four hundred dollars.

Donna studied the statement, then typed on a keyboard that looked hidden in the marble. "One is for The Point

Restaurant on the seventh floor and the other is your room charge. Would you like copies?" Dagger nodded. "Were you checking out?"

Sara picked up on it quickly. "We seemed to have misplaced our key cards."

"No problem." Her fingers flew across the keyboard, then tapped numbers on a small box, swiped a key card and placed it on the counter along with copies of the receipts.

The elevator deposited them onto the sixth floor. Dagger touched the Glock on his hip, wishing it were his Kimber and cursing the person who had stolen it.

"I thought walking into this place would jog some memory," Sara said. "What about you?"

"Nothing." Dagger paused in front of Room 619. A *Do Not Disturb* sign hung on the door. "Looks like someone slept in," he whispered.

Sara put her ear to the door and blocked out all sounds except for what was coming from the room. She heard a slight humming, possibly from a refrigerator. And another sound, a whirring, possibly the air conditioner. She stripped out those sounds and listened for footsteps, breathing. Some sign of human activity. She stepped back and shook her head.

Dagger slid the key card into the slot. The light turned green. Sara grabbed the handle and turned it while Dagger pulled out the Glock and charged in. The door clicked shut behind them. Sunlight spilled in from the opened drapes. Dagger turned on the bathroom light. Hotel toiletries looked unopened. The shower was dry, and clean towels were stacked on a rack above the toilet. There weren't any clothes hanging in the closet across from the bathroom. A small kitchenette contained a counter refrigerator, cabinet, sink, and a bar. The alcove opened to a sitting area with a widescreen television set, couch, chairs, and a desk. Dagger holstered the Glock.

Sara moved to the bedroom. One king size bed had its bedspread turned down, numerous pillows against the headboard. It didn't look slept in. Usually when they traveled out of town they reserved adjoining rooms or a two-bedroom suite. The thought appeared to be in both of their minds—either they had made the bed or they hadn't slept here. As though dismissing any of those thoughts, they quickly moved to the dresser.

Dagger pulled open the top drawer and breathed a sigh of relief. His wallet, keys, and the precious Kimber were there. He checked the contents of the wallet. "Credit cards, cash, drivers license. Everything is here."

Sara checked one of the other drawers and found a small, cream-colored purse. She checked the contents and found the Kel-Tec P32 Skizzy had given her along with her money and I.D. "Why would we leave all of this in the hotel room?" She walked over to the bedroom closet and opened the door. "My boots!" Cream-colored boots had been neatly placed on the floor. Her sweater and crop pants hung on a hanger next to Dagger's cargo pants and black shirt.

"It doesn't explain what else we were wearing. I doubt we walked out of here butt naked." Dagger took his clothes off of the hangers and started folding them.

"Maybe these were the clothes we wore last night and someone returned them to this room after they drove us to LaPorte." Sara grabbed the plastic laundry bag hanging in the closet and placed the folded clothes into it.

"That doesn't sound like something a normal kidnapper would do. Why take the chance of being seen on camera?"

"It doesn't make sense." After stuffing the rest of the possessions into the bag, they checked the garbage cans for notes, receipts, names scribbled on a notepad. Unfortunately, not one scrap of paper could be found that could give them a clue.

"Maybe we left our guns here and met someone for dinner." He reached into his pocket and pulled out the copies of receipts Donna had given him. "Are you hungry?"

7

"Hey, you two. Nice to see you again." The hostess set aside a stack of menus where she had inserted the daily specials. Sunlight streamed in from the wall of windows, making the gold threads in her dress shimmer. When she saw the puzzled looks on their faces, she added, "I'm Gayle. I seated you last night."

Dagger tried to nudge a memory cell, to find one ounce of recollection. Neither Gayle nor the spacious dining room with its nautical motif rang a bell. He handed her a receipt. "Can you tell me the name of my server?"

Gayle slipped a pair of bifocals on and studied the receipt. "Oh, Natalie worked that section. Did you find a problem with the charge?"

"Not at all. I just have a few questions for her, nothing to do with the service," Dagger said.

"She should be on duty in a half hour. Natalie is good at coming early to have a cup of coffee, change into her uniform. If you'd like to have a seat at the bar, I'll send her over."

"I wonder what we ate for that kind of money." Sara slipped onto a bar stool and looked around the restaurant. Each of the waitresses wore white shorts and a sequined bra under a blue sailor jacket. The waiters wore white pants, white shirts, and blue jackets.

The view from the wall of windows showed a spectacular sunset. Lights from boats blinked in the distance and a large ship could be seen headed for the harbor.

Dagger checked the room for cameras. He took a seat next to Sara and ordered a beer. The bartender no sooner set the bottle in front of him when a waitress sidled up to them.

"Gayle said you had a question about your bill." The name was appropriate seeing that her dark hair and eyes made her resemble Natalie Wood.

Not one thing about Natalie looked familiar. He wasn't sure how to approach the subject other than to tell the truth. He showed her the dinner bill and introduced himself and Sara.

"Neither one of us recalls being here Friday night. Can you fill in the blanks?"

Natalie swept her eyes from Dagger to Sara and back. "Really? That's strange because you didn't have that much to drink."

"With that large of a bill?" Sara couldn't believe food would cost that much.

"You did have mahi mahi and a couple appetizers." She turned to Dagger. "You had a twelve ounce filet, one of our most expensive pieces." She settled her gaze on the bill again. "You had a couple martinis. Your date had a tropical breeze. That's one of our specials."

"Who did we have dinner with?" Dagger asked.

Natalie shrugged. "Just the two of you."

Dagger nodded as though it all sounded familiar. However, not one thing she said, not one food or drink she had served, rang a bell.

"You don't remember any of this, do you?" Natalie looked puzzled, then shocked. "Did someone drug you?"

"That's what we're trying to figure out," Dagger confessed. "Have you had any problems in the past with a bartender or customer drugging someone?"

"No, not at all."

"Did we talk to anyone, perhaps at another table? Did anyone buy us a drink?"

"Not that I noticed. You had a table by the window, pretty much to yourself."

They thanked Natalie for her time, checked out of the hotel, and made their way across the lobby to the door. Sara clutched the laundry bag in her arms. "You do know how this looks, don't you?" she whispered. "Leaving a hotel with a laundry bag, no suitcase. I feel like a …"

"Hey, all I know is the night cost me six hundred bucks."

As they neared the concierge's desk, a man in a red and black palace guard uniform called out, "Did you enjoy that limo ride last night?"

Dagger approached the counter, his brain trying to conjure up some recollection of a limo. "We took a limo last night?"

"Well, yeah. I was outside when I heard the driver talking about seeing the meteor shower at the Dunes. Fred's the name." He reached out and shook Dagger's hand. "I went in for a few minutes. When I came back out you were both climbing in and the limo took off."

Dagger wasn't sure how to pull out more information without sounding like a whack job. "Did the limo have any markings on the side? I may have left my cell phone in the back seat."

Fred scratched his pink jaw. Either he had spent too much time under a sunlamp or his razor cut too close. "No, just a plain white stretch limo."

"What about the driver?" Sara asked. "What did he look like?"

"Oh…medium height, tuxedo, a hat most limo drivers wear, gray hair, handlebar moustache. Reminded me of an

English gentleman."

"Did we share the limo with anyone?" Dagger asked.

"No, just you two."

Dagger thanked him and pressed a fifty dollar bill into his hand. They left the hotel with a little more information, but not enough to fill in the important blanks.

Dagger sat in an Adirondack chair on the back deck, staring at the dark acreage, the garden going to seed. Solar landscaping lights cast a glow on the pond he had designed by the garden. The forest was alive with night sounds, and if he focused on the compact hedges by the fence, he could see yellow eyes staring back at him.

What kind of drug had been used on them and for what purpose? Had it been some type of truth serum? Had BettaTec abducted him to verify the chip in his neck still functioned? Why not just kill him rather than drive them to a cemetery, strip them, and place them in a coffin?

He cradled a beer in his hands as Sara took a seat next to him. She held a mug in her hand, steam drifting. She wore a flannel jacket yet Dagger hadn't felt the chill in the air. Anger fueled his body heat.

"You're thinking about BettaTec." Sara blew on the contents, then took a sip.

"Aren't you?"

Sara shook her head. "You already checked the satellites and they haven't moved."

BettaTec had two surveillance satellites circling the globe, keeping tabs on God knew what, confirming Skizzy's belief that Big Brother was watching. Except these weren't government satellites. Dagger believed BettaTec monitored and controlled the government as well as events happening around the world.

"I called Skizzy, told him to check any cameras in the vicinity of the hotel from last night. See if he finds the white limo, maybe catch a plate number."

"We obviously felt safe enough to climb into the limo, Dagger. If it had been anyone that set off your radar, we would have never climbed in. The driver probably gave us something to drink, something even my keen sense of smell couldn't detect."

"For what purpose? That's what's puzzling. We weren't robbed, beaten. We have all of our appendages. The only thing he could have been after would be information."

8

Padre Martinez mashed the gum in a practiced rhythm. He looked everywhere except the deceased's chest where Luther gathered organs as though picking vegetables at a farmer's market. Why did he have to eat breakfast this morning when he knew he'd have to view an autopsy?

"You obliterated his tats. Lotta ink there."

"You are lucky you didn't see the full landscape. Had Satan himself sitting on a throne, a naked lady giving him a lap dance. Beauty to behold," Luther said.

Padre shook his head. He let Luther continue his examination of the internal organs while he read the rap sheet on Diego Manuel. Three arrests for possession, assault with a deadly weapon, suspicion of distribution of illegal narcotics, and auto theft. Diego Manuel's life of crime started early when he lifted money from his fifth grade teacher's purse.

He set the reports down on the back counter as Luther waved a scalpel over the deceased's head. Sweat glistened on Luther's dark skin, even though it was chilly in the room. Luther Jamison had a slight build and a youthful face, despite the fact that he fast approached sixty.

Padre stepped closer, although once Luther started wielding the saw, he planned to stay a safe distance away to avoid the spray of blood. The blue gown he wore would protect his clothes, but just the thought of blood turned his stomach. Quite strange for a homicide detective.

"Nice car you found our friend in."

"Oh, yeah. Only had forty thousand miles on it," Padre said. "Still no sign of injury?"

The medical examiner had X-rayed the body and checked every crevice. He had yet to find a gun shot or knife wound. It appeared Diego just curled up in the trunk and died.

"Are you sure he didn't suffocate?"

Luther looked up from his carving duties. "Does this look like my first day on the job?"

"I'd never question your word, *amigo*. I'm just stumped is all. What about poison?"

"No undigested pills in the stomach. If he had used something, it would hopefully show up in the tox screen which could take weeks. Heart showed no signs of cardiac arrhythmia or defects. He was in relatively good health, considering his line of work."

Padre returned to the back counter, mashing his gum at a faster tempo as Luther pulled the scalp away from the skull in two flaps. He fired up the Stryker saw prompting Padre to add another stick of gum, as though chewing might drown out the sounds from the saw. He scanned the arrest record again just to keep his mind busy and off the sound of metal against bone.

The saw ground to a halt followed by a sound Padre hated even more—the sucking sound as Luther removed the cap to expose the brain. Then nothing. It became so quiet in the room that Padre could hear a slight drip of water in the sink on the other side of the room. He assumed Luther was busy removing the brain. *Why didn't I buy that bakery from Uncle Ramone?* he asked himself every time he stepped into Luther's house of horrors.

He waited for the sound of instruments clinking. A loud sigh could be heard followed by a "hmmm." Padre looked up from his notes to see Luther staring at the open cavity.

"This is interesting. I always knew you had to have half a brain to use or deal drugs."

Padre could swear Luther's dark skin had just turned a few shades lighter. "What's wrong?" Padre's feet appeared bonded to that one spot. He wasn't in any hurry to get closer. "Don't make me come over there, Lucy," Padre said in his best Ricky Ricardo impression.

Luther licked his lips and opened his mouth. The words hung in the air. "You better call Chief Wozniak."

9

"What did you find out?" Dagger stood in front of the monitor by his desk. Skizzy's face appeared in a small square on the upper right hand side of the screen.

"Just hold your horses. What do you think I am, a wizard?"

"WIZARD. WIZARD. HARRY POTTER," Einstein screeched.

Dagger stroked the macaw's back as it tap danced on the perch by the desk. "Quiet, Einstein."

Einstein let out a screech in protest.

"Hey, Einstein. Bite his ear for me, will you?" Skizzy pounded a few keys and a police report popped up on the screen. "This is the rap sheet on the deceased. Prints came back to a Diego Manuel. Name ring a bell?" Skizzy loved to hack the computers of any organization in authority and believed it only right since Big Brother watched our every move. He removed labels from all the canned goods he purchased because he felt Big Brother could scan the bar codes and know his choice of food and beverage. Paranoid schizophrenic barely scratched the surface of Skizzy's problems. Dagger liked to keep Skizzy busy so the little guy wouldn't go crazy.

"Never heard of him. What about trace evidence in the trunk and car?"

"Nothing has been put into their system yet. I thought

you'd like to know the guy's been lifting cars since age ten. It's possible he stole the Cadillac. Maybe you tossed him in the trunk and he suffocated."

"Thanks for that vote of confidence. What about known associates?"

"I'm sending you a copy of the report. I think I know of a hangout you might want to check out."

Dagger punched a key and Skizzy's ragged face disappeared. Within seconds the printer on his desk spewed out the report.

According to the report, the only known address for Diego Manuel appeared to be an empty lot on the east side of town. Names of relatives were non-existent. However, Skizzy had an address of another location. He never sold guns out of his pawn shop, except to Dagger and Simon. When a group of thugs tried to rob his shop, Skizzy had put the fear of God in them, then tailed them to a bar located in the main Hispanic community in Cedar Point.

"Leave your weapons in the car." Dagger opened a side compartment on the Navigator's side door, removed his ankle holster and placed it inside. Next he removed the Kimber and holster from his waist and tucked them into the foam interior. Sara handed him her Kel-Tec. Although he hated going anywhere unarmed, he wasn't about ready to have his guns confiscated. After parking the Lincoln Navigator two blocks away in the parking lot of a food store, they hoofed it to a bar down the street called *La Guarida del Diablo*.

"What the hell does that mean?"

"The Devil's Lair," Sara replied.

During a preliminary survey of the area, Dagger confirmed what Skizzy had said about the large warehouse attached to the back of the bar. Although graffiti had been painted on a number of the nearby buildings, it appeared as though the culprits knew not to come near The Devil's Lair.

As they approached the bar, two greasy looking thugs immediately took an interest. They probably didn't see too many *gringos* in this part of town. Sara's black leather pants hugged every curve and kept the guards' attention on her body before they noticed the hostile-looking stranger with her, someone whose tan and five o'clock shadow made him look more Middle Eastern, which usually garnered him a second and third search at airports. Sara smiled sweetly and Dagger could see the wheels spinning in their heads, wondering if this olive-skinned young woman with dark hair streaked with a variety of colors could be from their side of the border. Her turquoise eyes confused them, though, and it took a few seconds for them to realize the Beauty and the Beast were walking into their establishment.

Sara had been in dark bars before, but nothing like this. One lone candle sat on each table and only three on the bar. She blinked and switched to the eyesight of the hawk. She reached back and grabbed Dagger's hand, knowing it would take sometime for his eyes to adjust. Heat radiated from the customers, and she could see glowing stains on the pants of some of the males. Through a hawk's eye, urine usually glowed as though under an ultraviolet light.

As if assaulting their ears with loud music bleeding from the jukebox wasn't enough, they had to also withstand the greasy odors of tacos and fiery spices. Four men at the bar followed their progress while a woman in the corner stopped grinding her hips into a man's lap.

"You were right," Sara whispered. "Small restaurant and bar. There's a hallway to the right. The one to the left leads to the restrooms. And I think the kitchen is back there, too.

So the fun room must be this way."

A bruiser of a man standing behind the bar barked, "Are you lost?"

They ignored him and headed for the back of the room. "Does this place look familiar to you?" Dagger asked. His eyes still hadn't adjusted to the dark. If they had met the deceased and helped him in his journey to the hereafter, it was possible they had been here last night.

"Not at all." Sara reached a door which had a keypad. The hawk's visual acuity could make out the oils from the skin where the numbers had been punched. "Looks like only one number has been punched three times. Guess which number?" Sara started tapping the keypad.

"Six."

"You win the prize. Six-six-six."

Dagger shoved the handle down and they entered a well-lit warehouse, oblivious to the murmurs and commotion back in the bar. The door clanged shut behind them as Sara returned to her normal eyesight.

"What the…!" Chairs toppled over as a big man in a white suit and a shocked look on his face snapped his fingers. He pulled a foul smelling mini tree trunk from his mouth. "How did you get in here?" His voice boomed with a cottony cadence. The thin mustache on his upper lip looked penciled on.

The two approached as though they owned the place. A concrete palace had been created in the front part of the warehouse where an elaborate rug had been placed under a long table and chairs. Crates had been piled up to serve as walls. A bold striped silk drape served as a door, hiding whatever operation took place in the back portion of the warehouse. The men outside the bar had obviously neglected to let the big man know that he had unwanted guests.

"Search them," he bellowed as he yanked his throne chair back onto its legs and sat down. His crew of four were young and hadn't quite achieved the look of fierceness, let alone grown enough stubble to shave.

Two pudgy men in floral shirts advanced. Dagger knew the drill. He spread his arms and legs, but let his gaze take in the surroundings. Windows sat too high to give anyone a clear view from the outside. A thick scent of oil, dirt, and grease mixed with spicy food odors. Maybe the cigar smoke masked the odors of a meth lab. Besides the ornate table there were couches, a lamp, even a wide screen television. Dagger couldn't see a back door beyond the crates should he and Sara need it.

Large hands started manhandling him, rubbing his chest as though looking for a wire. One was getting friendly with his crotch while the other lifted each of his pant legs.

Dagger saw the hungry look on another man who eyed Sara as though he were on shore leave after five years out to sea. "If you touch her the same way, I'm going to come back here, break your arm and shove it so far up your ass you'll be able to scratch your head every time you take a step."

"You're pretty brave, my friend," Mister Cottonmouth said. He tossed a word over his shoulder. "Carlotta."

A woman materialized from behind the drape. Before the drape closed, Dagger caught a glimpse of a number of vehicles in the back room. Carlotta appeared to float rather than walk, and reminded Dagger of a gypsy witch who conjured spirits from their graves. Somehow her trim body supported the largest breasts he had ever seen. The top three buttons of her blouse had given up trying to contain the massive weight, and how the rest remained closed remained a mystery. Mister Cottonmouth watched her sway as she walked, long black hair kissing her hips. Her dark eyes seemed to settle on Dagger.

"The woman, Carlotta," the big man said with a chuckle. Dagger got the distinct impression Cottonmouth liked to watch her perform on another man, or woman, possibly at the same time.

She sidled up to Dagger and let her gaze crawl over his body. "Pity," she whispered in his ear. Then she turned her attention to Sara. Dagger expected to see jealous hatred in Carlotta's eyes, but his suspicions were confirmed as Carlotta placed her hands under Sara's jacket, worked her way from the back, around to the front. Slowly her hands ran under Sara's sweater. Dagger could swear every man in the place just sucked in a breath.

"Ummm, nice." Carlotta's words were like liquid silver.

Dagger didn't see tears of humiliation in Sara's eyes. Instead, she just stared at Carlotta with a slight smile. Carlotta may have thought Sara enjoyed the groping, but Dagger had seen that look before. It said, "Enjoy it now, 'cause if I ever get you alone I will rip you to shreds." As Carlotta worked her way down each pant leg, Sara glared at Cottonmouth who dabbed sweat from his forehead with a handkerchief.

Carlotta stepped back and looked at the two. "Embuerto, can we keep them?"

"Down girl." Embuerto broke out in a raucous laugh. Carlotta slinked behind Embuerto's chair.

The men stepped back and flanked Embuerto, guns at the ready. There were two on his left and two on his right, each armed with Tec-9s and twenty-round magazines. Embuerto had what looked like a Desert Eagle on his hip. Dagger doubted the chubby guy had ever seen the inside of a barracks.

"Now that we have become acquainted, let me say again. You have a lot of balls walking in here unarmed."

Dagger did a slow blink, bored with the game Embuerto was playing. "Who says I'm unarmed?"

10

Embuerto leaned forward slightly and placed his hand on the butt of his weapon. This appeared to be a signal as guns cocked and four Tec-9s were quickly leveled at Dagger. "Lucas, I thought you checked him thoroughly."

Dagger wondered if they had a chance of making it back the way they came without being shot. Two men with matching scars on their cheeks and matching shirts looked separated from birth. They had the same murderous hatred in their eyes.

"We did," Lucas said. "He doesn't have any weapons."

Dagger's grin widened as he jerked his head towards Sara. "She's my weapon."

Embuerto looked puzzled, then burst out laughing. As if on cue, his men followed suit. Before the last hiccup of an outburst, Embuerto snapped his fingers and the two porky twins produced knives. He snapped his fingers again and the knives came flying.

Sara took one step in front of Dagger and caught the knives by their handles. One reached a scant quarter of an inch in front of Dagger's cheek. The second one an inch from his chest.

"Cutting it close there, sweetheart." Dagger tried not to whoosh out a sigh of relief.

"Sorry, honey. It won't happen again." Sara flashed her innocent, sweet smile again as she twirled the knives.

A deadly silence had settled over the room. Dagger could swear he could hear dust settling in the crates.

Without breaking her smile, Sara flung the knives at Embuerto. They slammed into his chair seat, just barely missing the family jewels. Carlotta let out a scream. For a while Dagger thought Embuerto had swallowed his tongue. The portly guy sucked air as the knives vibrated from the speed and force of Sara's strength. His crew gawked at the quivering knives, too engrossed to notice that Sara had disarmed the two men to the right of Embuerto while Dagger disarmed the remaining two. A stunned silence blanketed the warehouse. Embuerto's men took a cautious step back when they saw Dagger pointing one of the Tec-9s at them.

"As I said." Dagger's smile had vanished and now his eyes took on that dark, sinister glare. If they had stepped closer, they would have seen that the irises had turned a smoky black, and something churned and moved behind them. "She's my weapon. Now, perhaps we can start over."

Embuerto grabbed the handle of one of the knives and pulled. The knife didn't budge. He tried a two-handed grip, sweat beading on his forehead. Sara walked over and pulled both knives out as though they were in butter instead of wood. She added them to the weapons on the floor.

Embuerto reached for his cannon. "Uh uh." Dagger shook his head, the Tek-9 aimed directly at the portly man who slowly removed his hand from the Desert Eagle.

"What is it you want?"

"For starters, you can put out that rancid smelling turd that smells like shit. My partner is allergic."

Embuerto held up the cigar. Carlotta took tentative steps and held out an ashtray for her man. He grabbed it and stubbed out the foul smelling log. He gave a nod to Sara. "My apologies. My wife is the same way." He set the ashtray on the table. "Now, what is so urgent that you had to hunt me down and terrorize my men to get my attention?" He peeled himself out of the chair, and Dagger wondered if Embuerto had wet himself. It was tough getting stains out of linen.

Dagger reached into his boot and pulled out a piece of paper. Embuerto glared at his men as he realized they didn't do as good of a search as he had demanded.

"What can you tell me about him?"

Embuerto studied the photo of Diego Manuel in the trunk of the Cadillac. Skizzy had retrieved the copy when he hacked into Padre's computer.

"Other than he's dead?"

"When did you see him last? What was he into other than drugs, weapons, and murder? Who does he hang out with other than you?"

"Such a laundry list. And why does Diego's death interest you?"

Dagger flashed a charming smile, the one he always used on his ex-fiancee, Sheila, when he wanted to wiggle out of something she wanted him to do. "Let's just say I'm a curious guy. Any idea how he ended up in the trunk of a car?"

"You seem to know a helluva lot more than we do."

"I doubt that."

"Are you working for the *predicador hombre*? Did he send you to find out where his eighty kilos are?"

"Huh?" Dagger turned to Sara.

"Preacher man," Sara explained.

"That's over two million dollars worth of coke, but we're not here about drugs. Where did Diego go Friday night?"

Embuerto heaved a long sigh. Given his size, Dagger wondered if the big guy was having a heart attack. "He had to drive *predicador* somewhere."

Sara asked, "Why is he called Preacher?" A dreamy look

crossed Carlotta's face. Dagger had the distinct impression this Preacher had heard her confession a time or two.

"Scar," Embuerto said. "He has a scar of a cross on his forehead." He used his finger and made the sign of the cross on his own forehead. "Preacher went to dinner somewhere."

"The Point Restaurant at the Ritz Hotel," Carlotta offered.

Embuerto glanced over his shoulder at his main squeeze who quickly looked away.

"Now we're getting somewhere," Dagger said, more under his breath. "Does this guy use a limo?"

"Nah." Embuerto brushed that comment aside. "Big SUV. Black, like his heart." He checked his throne chair to make sure the knives were gone before sitting down. He grasped the arms and settled back. "I'm done here. Unless you's the police, I don't have to tell you another damn thing."

Dagger studied Embuerto's rag tag group. He didn't concern himself much with drug gangs. Couldn't care less if they knocked each other off. He hated when they pushed their shit on kids, though, and what they did to a society with an "if it feels good, do it" mentality.

Dagger's cell phone chirped, indicating he had a text message. Padre's text read, *Meet me at the morgue ASAP.* "Oh shit."

He shoved the phone back in his pocket. "We'll leave your toys. I think you are going to need as much protection as possible."

Embuerto motioned with his chin, giving a peek at what had been a non-existent neck. "How did Diego die?"

"Cops don't know yet. If I find out, I'll let you know so you can be prepared. You may be next. Now, where does this guy hang out?"

"Anywhere and everywhere. Never stays in the same place more than once. Now get the hell out of my establishment."

They turned to leave the same way they came when Embuerto yelled, "HEY!"

Dagger and Sara turned to see him pointing the Desert Eagle at them, a murderous glare in his eyes. He pulled the trigger. *Click.*

Sara opened her hand to reveal the clip she had removed from Embuerto's gun.

Dagger tsked. "And here I thought we were getting along so well."

11

"Do you think they found some trace of us in the car or on the body?" Sara whispered as they made their way from the reception area to the examining room.

"Padre could have talked to us at home or in his office. For some reason, he wanted us in the morgue." Dagger pounded through the door and into the examining room. "Well, aren't you a sorry bunch." Luther, Padre, and John Wozniak clustered behind the head of the body that resembled the man taken from the trunk of Skizzy's Cadillac.

Padre sighed while Chief Wozniak's eyes admired Sara's tight-fitting leather slacks. Being on his third wife, Wozniak always had an eye for a beautiful woman.

"Hope you don't want us in gowns and booties. Blue isn't my color."

"Hello to you, too, Dagger," Wozniak said. "How I've missed you." He turned his attention to Sara. "On the other hand, I could look at you all day."

It had been a long day, or two. Maybe three. And still he was no closer to discovering who had drugged them and stuffed them in a coffin. He couldn't ask Padre if he had sent him on a mission. Leave it up to his partner to do the digging.

"How long has it been, Chief?" Sara asked. "Padre?"

"Too long. If I had my way, I'd want a daily dose." While the chief of detectives played cop with the hots, Dagger could see that Padre's skin had taken on a pallid sheen. Since Padre hadn't replied with, "We had lunch yesterday," Dagger could only assume the cop hadn't sent him to babysit the victim.

"What's up? I'm bushed and in need of sleep." Dagger studied the body of Diego Manuel. Just a kid who still had acne. A tattoo of a devil decorated his left shoulder while a tattoo of an angel adorned the other.

"This the body found in the trunk of a Cadillac?"

"How did you know that?" Padre had finally found his tongue.

"Police scanner," Sara quickly replied.

Padre ran down the abbreviated history of Diego Manuel, concentrating mainly on where his body had been found. Dagger expected him to ask if they had ever seen him before or to report that his and Sara's prints had been found in the car, which would have been impossible since their prints weren't on file.

"As you can tell," Padre said, waving a hand over the naked remains, "no visible wounds. Not even a mosquito bite."

Dagger took his time surveying the body as Padre spoke. He had to agree. Diego hadn't suffered any trauma. "Okay." He let the word hang out, still not sure why he and Sara had been called.

Chief Wozniak curled his finger and motioned them to their tight cluster. Dagger and Sara exchanged confused looks, then joined them at the head of the table. The skull cap had been removed, the brain cavity exposed. Padre picked up a pen light and aimed it at the cavity. It glistened stark white, as though Luther had rinsed it in bleach.

"Nice job, Luther."

"I didn't do anything," Luther said. "It came that way, right from the factory."

"Whoa, the doc has a sense of humor." Dagger didn't hear

anyone laughing. He noticed Padre's jaw chewing furiously while Chief Wozniak's face blazed red as the hair on his head. Even his bulbous nose appeared to be flashing red.

"There wasn't a brain," Padre finally explained.

Dagger scratched his five o'clock shadow as though in deep thought. Sara bent down to examine the nose and ears closer. "Maybe someone sucked it out through the nose, like they did to mummies," Sara suggested.

Luther shook his head. "There would have been some residue in the nose and sinus cavity, not to mention inside the skull itself."

"Killers are getting neat these days." Again, Dagger's humor was met with silence. "Who owns the Cadillac?"

"We ran the plates," Padre said. "Reported stolen over fifteen years ago. The plates were registered to a Buick so someone did some fancy swapping of plates. Can't decipher the vehicle I.D. number. Analysts will see if they can restore any part of it. I'm not holding my breath. And before you ask, no. We didn't find any brain residue in the trunk. Had to have died somewhere else and his body dumped in the trunk."

"So." Dagger shifted his gaze from Padre to Wozniak. "You want us to find his brain?"

Wozniak balled his mitt-sized hands into fists. He had little patience with Dagger's humor. His town used to be pretty quiet until Dagger moved in. Then it morphed into *Little Twilight Zone on the Prairie*. From a serial killer who could shapeshift into a werewolf to a killer who could make himself invisible, and the latest, a time warp which opened during a solar burst and a rare lightning storm, the crazies seemed to have followed Dagger to Cedar Point.

"The killer had to have some medical experience," Sara suggested. "How else could he know exactly where..." She suddenly realized *cut* wouldn't be an appropriate word since the body didn't have any incisions.

"He didn't happen to die before and come back to life as a, you know." Dagger didn't even crack a smile at his own suggestion.

"Please don't tell me you were going to say zombie." Wozniak pressed his hands on either side of his skull to keep his own head from exploding. He turned to his sergeant. "You deal with him." He glanced quickly at Sara. "How do you ever put up with him?"

"It's a daily chore."

"So." Dagger gave the men his full attention. "What are we really doing here?"

Luther put the body parts back together, then pulled the sheet over Diego's remains. "Whenever I come across anything that I have never encountered in my thirty plus years in forensics, I look to someone else's area of expertise. You deal in weird," he told Dagger. "I'm open to any ideas."

"I'm not," Wozniak huffed under his breath.

Dagger had yet to figure out how Diego ended up in the trunk of Skizzy's Cadillac. "Find anything else in the car?"

Luther's laugh halted when he noticed Wozniak's cold glare. "You obviously haven't been watching the news." The chief actually showed a little embarrassment. "These damn reporters with their cameras. And to add insult to injury you have these assholes with their cell phones. We're the laughing stock of the country, letting some dog…"

"Wolf," Padre corrected him.

Sara avoided Dagger's eyes.

"Anyway, a damn wolf goes and snatches one of the evidence bags and takes off."

Luther stifled another laugh. "It's had two million hits on *YouTube*."

Sara had to remind herself to breathe. She could feel the rage flowing from Dagger's body.

Dagger finally found his voice. "What was in the bag?"

"Hair sample," Padre said. "Long. Couldn't have belonged to the deceased so I have a feeling Diego had a girlfriend in the car. She could be a witness to whoever or whatever killed him."

"Whatever?" Sara didn't like the sound of that. She was glad she had pulled her hair back in a long braid, as if that could hide the length and color from Padre's experienced eyes.

Padre gave a shrug of his shoulders. "Possible this could be some gang war, fight over turf, a message being sent to Diego's boss. Who knows? My main concern is the method used. How does someone remove a brain without any trace?"

"New type of drug?" Dagger tried not to think about the two men BettaTec had sent who had some type of bomb placed inside of them. They had literally blown up when their missions were complete.

"I know of no drug that could target just one organ. Not unless someone has found a new designer drug." Luther gave that more thought as he rolled Diego's gurney into one of the coolers and slammed the door shut. "Even if someone laced his cocaine with something unique I would see traces of the cocaine. And my best guess is it wouldn't have been instantaneous."

"Well, it has been several hours since the body was discovered," Wozniak offered. "Maybe some type of hydrochloric acid was added to the cocaine."

"That's a thought," Padre said. "Maybe made some type of acid into a powder or crystal and when they snorted it, the brain disintegrated."

"Again, his entire nasal cavity would be gone." Luther

stripped off the blue gown and tossed it in a receptacle. "I admit, I'm stumped, which is why we hoped Dagger could come up with an explanation."

"Sorry, can't help you."

"Just keep your eyes and ears open," Wozniak said. "After all, you seem to have a direct line to the weird and really weird."

Sara tried the hawk vision again in an attempt to see if she had missed something, but if the best medical examiner couldn't find a logical explanation, who could? "It's as though the brain just evaporated."

12

Dagger called Skizzy as he pulled away from the curb. He no sooner explained the missing brain then Skizzy said, "Aliens. I told you they are here. Look just like you and me."

"This is serious, Skizzy. Give me another explanation."

"Well, if there's some new drug out there, I haven't heard about it. I need some time to hack websites."

"What about the Cadillac? Can you tell where it's been since it left your garage?" Skizzy's underground warehouse served as a garage and could be accessed from a hidden entrance in the back of the pawn shop. Skizzy only allowed Dagger in his warehouse.

"I told you. No can do. Other than finding my Cadillac where you parked it, I can't tell you where it's been."

"What about the hotel? There have to be cameras in the parking lot."

"Nada."

"Then check nearby streets and look for a black SUV. This Diego kid would have been driving a guy with a cross on his forehead."

"What about my Cadillac?"

"See if the camera shows me arriving in the Cadillac. If I left in the limo, I must have come back for it. Although according to Padre, Diego cut his teeth on stealing cars."

"You owe me a car. I liked that Cadillac."

"Steal it from the impound and have it repainted."

"Yeah, right. Like I can ever do that."

Dagger pushed the end button on the console. "I hate the fact that I have a chunk of my life unaccounted for."

"I would think by now you would be used to it." Sara started to laugh at her comment, then saw the look on Dagger's face. "You still think BettaTec is behind our kidnapping?"

"Until I have another explanation, that's all I have to go on."

He admired the waterfront scenery in Vancouver, British Columbia. The Pacific Rim had unobstructed views of the water and mountains, and could be accessed by plane or his private yacht. Staying in five star hotels garnered some privacy, and registering under one of his many aliases assured him anonymity with his adversaries. Behind him quick fingers tapped on a keyboard. Fredrik Hensen had been his personal assistant for the past decade, having acquired the task after the untimely death of his previous assistant whose allegiance had been purchased for the right price. It was Fredrik who would make all reservations and correspondence as though he were the one in charge.

"Mister Keyes, I have the uplink." Fredrik vacated the chair and held it back while Keyes sat down. "Just press this button, Sir."

This had been the one email he had been waiting for the past six months. He opened the email and read the message:

Test results are attached. Video feed lasts for twenty-five seconds.

He pressed the arrow and watched. Open land, plenty of sand and cacti screamed desert. By the looks of the mountains he would guess the Southwest in the United States. A man had been bound to a chair in front of a concrete fence. Eyes wide behind horn-rimmed glasses first showed anger then fear. Although the video lacked sound, the man screamed at someone not revealed by the camera. He struggled against the restraints, but his efforts appeared fruitless. Then the eyes looked puzzled, widened in shock. After five seconds his body started to shake, his head appeared rigid, fixed in place by something not immediately noticeable.

At ten seconds the victim's eyes appeared to bulge and his body vibrated as though hit with an electric charge. At fifteen seconds the body fell slack against the chair back.

"Amazing," Fredrik whispered from behind him.

"Yes," Keyes replied as he checked his Jaeger-Lecoultre Gyrotourbillion watch, a mere seven hundred thousand dollar gift to himself. He loved its intricate dials and numbers, and the fact that gravity could not affect the accuracy. "What do you think, Fredrik? This video is a month old already."

"I'd say he's already opened the bidding and not one person has offered the amount he is looking for. So he has come to the person with the deepest pockets."

"Yes, I believe you are right." He typed out a response:

I noticed your video feed is already a month old. I need more current tests before I commit and I need to inspect the merchandise. The effect also takes too long. Cut it in half, then get back to me.

The response was immediate:

Will have more video for you soon.

He signed off and closed the lid on the laptop. "I have

a feeling he has already improved his product and probably aims to double the price. Mason Godfrey is one man who should never be trusted."

13

Padre smelled her perfume before she crossed his threshold. A steno pad hit his desk followed by a well-rounded cheek draped on the corner, the short skirt exposing a lot of skin.

"Thought you were at a spa retreat with your mother."

"I have to take my mother in small bites. Three months would have been far too long so I figured four weeks was enough to keep me in the will." Sheila tapped manicured nails on the desktop. "What's shaking, my cute little taco."

Sheila Monroe worked as an investigative reporter for the *Daily Herald*, one of the many newspapers her father, Leyton Monroe, owned. Her R and R trip helped to clear her mind of things she had seen at the Sebold mansion. Sheila had disappeared for three days after accompanying a ghost hunting group's foray into the unknown.

Padre was certain Luther would keep a lid on the information about the brainless body in the morgue. Luther ran a pretty tight ship and had been careful not to mention the missing brain in his official report. Until they discovered the who and how, this one detail would not be unleashed on the public. So what exactly Sheila had been hearing through the grapevine made him curious.

"You know, this and that. What about you? All healed after that ghost hunting expedition?"

"It has certainly cured me of spending the night in a haunted house. I still have weird dreams and unanswered questions. Keep seeing this guy in turn-of-the-century clothes. Would have been good looking if he didn't have serial killer eyes. Like I said, weird." She did that head shake some women do and flipped strands of platinum hair away from her face. Sheila looked rich, from her designer suits to her expensive hairstyle to the fancy cars she changed on a monthly basis.

Padre tapped his keyboard as a hint that he had more important things to do. He had been having a tough time finding any of Diego Manuel's relatives. Even a call to Mexico resulted in a laundry list of Manuel's, including his contact on the Mexican police force. As far as anyone knew, Diego snuck across the border in his youth and used someone else's name, possibly a fellow illegal who died crossing the desert.

"Anything to report on the body found in the Cadillac's trunk?"

"Do you have any idea how many people with the surname of Manuel live in Mexico? You would think someone, a parent or some relative would be missing this guy. So if I have *nada*, you get *nada*."

Sheila slid off of the desk and took a seat in a worn upholstered chair. Her cat-ate-the-canary smile that she wore told him she knew something he didn't.

"What are you doing working a possible gang killing? Don't have any high society weddings to cover?"

"Oh, pulleeze. You know I've been covering crime in our lovely town. And with the influx of gangs and drugs, I'm hardly at a loss for front page news."

"What could you possibly know about the drug trade?"

"Well, golly gee, where do I start?" Sheila placed a hand on each of her cheeks and feigned the wide-eyed innocence of an eighth grader. She crossed her arms as though bored.

"Heroin, cocaine, bath salts. And meth has so many cute names like crank, ice, bikers coffee, hillbilly crack. I especially like that one."

"Okay, okay. So you can read. You want to follow the drug crumb trail, go see Sanders with the county drug task force. Be warned. The drug gangs are in it for the big bucks and they carry big guns."

"How sweet. You're worried about me."

Padre leaned back in his chair and studied the attractive debutante. She could have been a runway model in her youth or married to a duke or prince. Instead, she placated her father's wishes to one day own his cadre of newspapers.

"I'm impressed. You've done your homework." He tapped a pen on the notepad as he contemplated how much to share with the reporter. "Hear of any new designer drugs out there?"

"Is that what you think killed him?"

"Don't have the tox screen back yet. Could be something unique."

A perfect eyebrow lifted. One had to be careful around Sheila. "Unique how?"

"Not sure yet, other than the victim didn't show the usual signs of a drug overdose. When the results aren't noticeable and there aren't visible wounds and knowing the deceased ran with a drug cartel, we can only assume they are moving something…unique. Maybe he either sampled the merchandise or offered to be a guinea pig." Padre opened a file folder, pulled out a photo and slid it across the desk. "The deceased had a tattoo of an angel and a devil, one on each of his shoulders. Don't think those are quite the symbol of a gang." He slid a second photo across the desk.

"Wow. How degenerate. The devil getting a lap dance. Definitely not a symbol of any gang."

"Any idea who the best tat artists are? That took a bit of time to do and, although I hate to say it, the detail is fantastic."

"Do you have any tats, Padre?"

Padre caught the seductive glare in her green eyes. Sheila couldn't help herself. She knew she was beautiful and believed every man desired her. "Actually no, but I bet you have a few."

Her eyes said, *and I bet you'd like to see them.* "Dagger always hated my, what he called, tramp stamp."

Padre wasn't about ready to get caught up in the love lost tales of Sheila Monroe. He slid another photo across the desk. "This is the car where we found Diego's body. Looks like a dump site. He wasn't killed there that we can tell. So perhaps he did sample too much of the merchandise and his buddies had to get rid of the body."

Sheila picked up the photo and studied it. "Nice wheels. Did you find the owner?"

"License plates were stolen, serial number removed. We are trying to retrieve some of the numbers." He noticed the look on her face.

Her lips slightly parted. "He was found in this Cadillac?"

"Yeah, why?"

Sheila shook her head. "No reason. My daddy owned one of these years ago, before he discovered Beemers, Mercedes, and Lexus." She set the photos down and checked her watch. "Well, I'm sure we can both agree on one thing." She stood and flung a purse the size of an overnight bag over her shoulder. "He didn't put himself in that trunk."

14

Dagger's phone buzzed. He checked the name on the screen and groaned. Sheila. He punched the speaker button and moved away from the desk as though it were dangerous to stand too close to the sound of her voice.

"Sheila. Calling me from that palatial spa you are staying at?"

"Lucky for you, darling, I'm home and hard at work."

Dagger wasn't sure how much poking and prodding to do, but he had to find out if she had any memories of the Sebold mansion.

"Did the mud baths and hot rock therapies work?"

"If you are asking if I still look great, of course." After a slight pause she asked, "Do you have me on the speaker?"

"Absolutely. I need witnesses to everything you say to me."

"AWWKKK, WICKED WITCH OF THE WEST." Einstein screeched his disapproval of Dagger's ex-fiancee. When they were engaged, Sheila had pressured Dagger to get rid of Einstein, something he had refused to do. Dagger turned to see Sara closing the door to the aviary.

"I just wanted to tell you I made dinner reservations for seven o'clock at Pierre's. We need to talk."

"We're talking now."

"Not over the phone. In person."

"Why?"

An exaggerated sigh burst from the speaker phone. Then she explained how she had talked to Padre about Diego Manuel and how she had seen a photo of the Cadillac where the body had been found.

Dagger waited for more. When Sheila seemed to exhaust all of her explanation, he asked, "And?" He checked his watch. Not that he had anything else to do, other than piece together one missing day of his life.

"I'll tell you at dinner."

"You'll tell me now or I'm hanging up."

Another long, exasperated sigh. "All right. When Padre showed me the picture of the Cadillac, I realized it's the same car I saw you driving in Friday night. Same color, same license plate number."

Sara and Dagger locked eyes.

"I don't own a Cadillac," Dagger said.

"I took your photo with my cell phone."

"Why would you do that?" Dagger could almost hear her shrug through the speaker.

"I don't know. Maybe for posterity."

"You're stalking me."

"Oh, please. I have more important things to do. However, these days whenever there is a body in the news, your name seems to be attached. So dinner at Pierre's."

"Too expensive. Meet me at the Harborside Restaurant in twenty." He hung up just as he heard her say, "that dive?"

Dagger found her seated at a table by the window. He could swear she must have had some enhancements done while at that expensive spa. Her eyebrows appeared to have been lifted and her cleavage increased. She had always been stunning. Flawless make-up, debutante looks, pampered and spoiled. How he ever let her get her claws into him, he'll never fully understand. One too many drinks one night and before he knew it she was flashing an engagement ring. She never had and never would forgive him for not showing up at their rehearsal dinner. He had met Sara and the two helped break up a theft ring operating out of the Cedar Point Police Department. Completely forgot the dinner, although Simon claims Dagger had been too distracted. Although Sheila's father doubted the wedding would take place, heaven help the man who dared to leave his daughter at the altar and expect to walk away unscathed. Leyton Monroe turned up a lot of rocks to find something in Dagger's background. The only history Leyton could find had been invented by Skizzy. Dagger had been in Daddy's crosshairs ever since.

Dagger pulled out a chair and sat down. Sheila's eyes lit up as her gaze ran over his body, until she saw Sara pull out a chair and sit down.

"I thought I said to come alone."

"Where I go, Sara goes. She's my bodyguard."

Sheila would have laughed had she not been busy admiring Dagger's dangerous appeal. He was the bad boy her father had always warned her against. "Can't trust yourself when I'm around. How flattering."

"Right. Can't trust myself not to wring your neck. Now show me the picture."

"Gee, can't we order a drink first? We have a lot to catch up on."

Sara drilled him with a glare that said to play nice.

A waitress set menus on the table and pulled a pencil from her apron. "What can I get you to drink?"

Dagger ordered three Bloody Marys.

"Aren't you going to card her?" Sheila asked. She usually wouldn't be seen in a restaurant that didn't have waiters in tuxedos; and just by the lifting of her chin and nose, Sheila had just broadcast her disdain of what she considered nothing more than a café by a boat club. To Sheila it contained nothing more than small fishing boats and thirty foot cruisers, for crissake. The yacht club, where her family owned a real yacht, would never rent a dock space to any boat smaller than forty feet. And God forbid if the Cedar Point Yacht Club hired any waitress named Blanche. Sheila assumed she had a second job at a truck stop the way she had her pencil jammed into the bun at the nape of her neck.

"She's with Dagger so she's okay. You have any other complaints?"

Sheila pulled back her shoulders. "I'd like to speak to the manager."

Dagger sighed. Blanche said, "You're looking at her." Blanche smiled at Sara. "Three drinks coming up."

Sheila's cheeks flushed as Blanche walked away. Her eyes shifted to Sara. She ran a cursory glance from her face void of makeup, her dazzling turquoise eyes, her leather jacket and black cargo pants. "He even has you dressing like him."

Blanche brought their drinks, then took their orders. Sheila appeared to sniff her drink first before taking a dainty sip.

"It isn't well water, Sheila." Dagger removed the celery stalk from his drink and handed it to Sara.

"In this place I wouldn't doubt they siphoned it from the lake." Sheila ignored Sara as she spoke, which didn't bother Sara in the least. And Sheila spoke with her hands, at least one hand, the one where she still flashed Dagger's engagement ring. At least she now wore it on her right hand instead of her left, possibly something her current boyfriend demanded.

Blanche returned with a tray and distributed their lunch. Sara had ordered a shrimp salad, Dagger a burger, and Sheila a Caesar salad. Sheila made small talk, dragging out her reason for the meeting. After finishing half of his burger, Dagger couldn't wait any longer.

"The photo, Sheila. I want to see it, especially if someone is impersonating me."

"I highly doubt that. I know every inch of you, Chase Dagger." She said it with a smile as she dug into her purse.

Dagger reached across the table and pulled the photo from Sheila's grasp. His face showed nothing that he would want Sheila to easily interpret. Dagger showed the photo to Sara.

"When and where did you take this?" Sara asked.

"Not so fast." Sheila set her fork down and took another sip of her drink.

Sara handed the photo back to Dagger.

"Cut to the chase, Sheila."

"No pun intended," Sheila added with a smug smile.

"Yes, that's me in the car. No, the car isn't mine and no, I did not kill the guy in the trunk." *That I know of,* Dagger thought.

"So how did he get in it? Tell me what you do know?"

Sara continued eating, preferring to listen and people-watch. The tables by the windows quickly filled with patrons eager to view the sunset. The restaurant served more blue collar workers and fisherman rather than yacht owners and country club elite who frequented the Cedar Point Yacht Club.

"Dagger, you're stalling." A notepad and pen materialized next to Sheila's plate.

"Sara." The word no sooner left his mouth then Sara pulled Sheila's purse from the back of her chair.

"Hey!"

Dagger made a quick scan of the restaurant. "Keep your voice down. You don't think I'm going to talk if I know you have a recorder in your purse."

Sara did a search, unzipping a makeup bag, checking side pockets. Then she pulled out a small recorder and handed it to Dagger.

"Nice." Dagger pressed a button. "You had it on record." He pressed erase, then shoved it in his pocket.

"Can't blame a reporter for trying."

They waited for Blanche to remove the empty plates before continuing.

"Let's start with where you were when you saw me, what time was it, what day?"

Sheila huffed at her inability to control the discussion. "Around seven."

"Be more specific."

Now Sheila's reporter radar kicked into high alert. "Okay. I picked up my prescription about five to seven and I had a little more shopping to do at Walgreens. I was standing on the curb when I saw you pull up to the stop light in the Cadillac. I found it strange that you would be driving an old man car, something my father owned when I was a kid."

"The street, Sheila. Which Walgreens?" Dagger snapped.

"The one on Water Street. You were headed north." She flicked her gaze to Sara. "With her."

"How was I dressed, could you tell?"

"How were you dressed? How could you not remember what…?"

"Just tell me. Casual? Sportcoat? Tux?"

"Right, like I could ever get you in a tux. You were dressed the way you're always dressed—all black, leather jacket, no tie. I don't know about Sara." She looked again at the two, this time the suspicion even stronger.

"So I was headed north, toward the lake, possibly the Ritz Hotel?"

"Oh please. Why on earth would you go to a hotel?" Then her smile faded as she glanced from Dagger to Sara and back to Dagger. She cleared her throat, then took a long swig of her drink. "That's a pretty expensive hotel."

"They have a nice restaurant," Sara said, although she would rather let Sheila stew in her own suspicions.

"Yes, they do." Sheila didn't hide her relief as she turned her attention back to Dagger. "Now, until you explain why you were in a dead man's car and why you don't remember that night, I'm just going to add a few little details into my headline story. I might even include a photo or two."

Dagger flagged down Blanche and ordered a beer. Neither Sara nor Sheila wanted another drink. Dagger waited for his beer, weighing his options on how much to tell his ex. With the way the last few days had been going, he didn't have much choice.

"We were drugged," Dagger stated. "I don't remember much of that night. All I know is we woke up in a coffin in LaPorte. I found my wallet, weapons, everything in our hotel room." He avoided mentioning the missing clothes.

Whatever relief had shown on Sheila's face evaporated with the words *hotel room*. She ran her right hand through her platinum hair as though flashing her engagement ring meant something to Dagger. "So, how did you end up with a Cadillac?"

"I supposedly borrowed it from a friend. He noticed it missing."

"Must be that squirrelly guy with a conspiracy theory behind every spaceship." Sheila put her pen down and leaned her elbows on the table. "Have you been able to figure anything out?" She suddenly acknowledged Sara's presence. "Wait. They put each of you in a coffin?"

"In the same coffin." Sara caught herself before mentioning that they were both naked. "We didn't know if we were buried under six feet of dirt or sitting on the bottom of Lake Michigan."

"Wow." A shiver ran through Sheila's body as though some memory of the Sebold mansion had suddenly come to mind. "What else?"

Dagger told her about the dinner charge on his credit card which was how he knew he had eaten there Friday night. "The concierge described the limo driver we supposedly left with. I can only assume Diego jacked the Cadillac. What happened to him after that, I haven't a clue. I didn't find any information in my office on current cases. Not even a phone number or message on my answering machine. All I found was the charge on my credit card."

Sara caught Blanche whizzing past the table and ordered an iced tea. Sheila ordered another Bloody Mary, a double this time.

Once they received their drinks and Blanche left, Sheila asked, "The body in the trunk, you're sure you never met him before?"

"Positive."

Sheila turned to Sara. "What about you? Maybe he made too many lustful glances at you and Dagger got pissed."

Sara didn't know how to respond to that. She kept sipping her tea.

"Well." Sheila reclaimed the photo and jammed it in her purse. "This has been interesting. You two would have been the last to see the deceased."

Dagger glared at Sheila over the rim of his beer glass. He remembered all too well that his ex was a great manipulator, and he would never forget how her previous front page stories had hinted at questionable actions by both Sara and Padre, practically accusing each of them of murder or theft. To Sheila game-playing was a sport, but he refused to be caught up in it.

The silence stretched which made Sheila noticeably uncomfortable. She pulled out her compact to freshen her makeup. If her goal was to blackmail Dagger, she wouldn't do it in front of Sara. "Padre says Diego could have died of a drug overdose," she said as she repaired her lipstick. "Seems strange that our illustrious medical examiner has yet to find a cause of death."

Except that something or someone sucked out his brain, Dagger thought. He wasn't about ready for that detail to make front page news.

15

"Socko. Who's on duty with you tonight?" Embuerto turned the key in the dead bolt, then punched a code into the security system, reminding himself to change the code tomorrow since the stranger and that scary girlfriend of his had managed to gain access to the warehouse.

Carlotta opened a compact and studied her makeup in the mirror. "You need more lights back here, Embuerto. I can barely see my eye shadow."

"It's supposed to be dark. You want everyone to see how to enter the warehouse? Perhaps you want a spotlight on the door and a note with the alarm code."

"Socko." Embuerto slapped the skinny kid on the back of the head. "A name."

Socko pulled his eyes away from Carlotta's cleavage. "Uh, Cannibal. He's running a little late."

Embuerto didn't want to ask how Cannibal got his nickname. "We'll wait for him together. I want two men here at all times. He knows better than to be late. One more incident and he's fired."

"I'm hungry, Embuerto." Carlotta snapped her compact closed and shoved it in her purse.

"You are always hungry."

"And I want to go dancing." She started swaying her hips, and smiled as Socko's eyes followed every move.

"Food, yes. Dancing, no. You want to dance, you can

dance for me at home." Embuerto shoved his fists somewhere in the vicinity of his hips and surveyed the alley entrance.

"Oh, Embuerto. You know I like an audience when I dance. You fall asleep or you get on the phone and ignore me. Please, baby."

The big man tried to speak, to get his tongue to work. He couldn't blink or even get his lips to move. It was as though someone had cut the circuit breaker in his brain. He couldn't move his arms or legs either. A white light flashed before his eyes and he wondered if he were having a stroke. He had heard that people see their departed relatives standing in a light, beckoning them to join, to climb the staircase to Heaven. In his case, there might be a trapdoor to Hell before he reached the staircase. Maybe if Carlotta could call for an ambulance, the EMTs could save him, could get him to a hospital in time.

He couldn't get the words out. Suddenly, the back lot tilted in slow motion and he felt an intense pain in his head. The pavement came up quickly and Embuerto bounced like an overstuffed piñata.

"EMBUERTO!" Carlotta knelt down next to the prone body and clasped his hand as his body twitched and jerked. "DO SOMETHING," she yelled. But the kid just stared in horror, mouth dropping open. Embuerto stopped moving and his body settled slowly, his eyes taking on a dazed look.

In the crisp night air with temperatures hovering around fifty, the two stared in shock as wisps of steam gradually drifted from Embuerto's ears and nose. Then ever so slowly the steam leaked from the pupils of his eyes.

Both Carlotta and Socko screamed and tore down the alley.

* * *

Sara checked the time on the clock radio on her nightstand. Three in the morning. She didn't know what woke her, probably the dreams. Dressed in an Indianapolis Colts jersey and a pair of shorts, Sara stopped outside her room and stared at the living room below. The windows reached to the peak of the second floor, the blinds not always closed in the evening. She made her way across the catwalk that dissected the living room and stood staring out of the windows. Clouds sulked in front of a moon so full it lit up the back acres. Her eyes searched the tree line for signs of movement. A fence surrounded the three hundred acres and there was an alarm at the gate. If anyone gained access over the fence, a motion detector would set off another alarm. All of the security measures had been installed by Dagger.

She made her way to the kitchen to find Dagger drinking a cup of coffee at the granite table, the light above the stove casting the only light in the room.

"You couldn't sleep either," Dagger said.

She took a cup from the cabinet and poured herself some coffee. "First I dreamed of being trapped one mile below the ground in a coffin, and the next I was being chased in the woods by a beast with three rows of teeth." She pulled out a chair and sat down.

"Strange. We must be sharing dreams."

When Skizzy had discovered the chip in Dagger's neck, he had found a series of numbers imprinted on the case. Dagger recognized them as coordinates and it led him to a town in Nebraska, one mile below the surface. He had lived and been trained in that underground lab. Trained to be a killer with orders delivered via the chip in his neck. Repressed memories were recovered by a Konrad computer named Connie, a computer altered by Dagger's mother specifically to give him back his memory should he ever return. But the facility self-destructed nearly killing him and Sara before all of his memories of his time at BettaTec could be revealed. Dagger never knew his real name, only a number—six one seven. The name, Chase Dagger, had been a spark of inspiration after escaping BettaTec.

"What if we go to a hypnotist," Sara suggested. "It could help us remember who drugged us."

Dagger studied her over the rim of his cup. She was a far cry from the eighteen-year-old who had walked into his office over two years ago, a young woman who had looked like she had stepped out of some island waters with her almond shaped eyes, bronzed skin, and exotic features. She had been as skittish as a kitten, but boy, had times changed.

"Once they put you under, Sara, you have no control. The shrink could ask me about my past. Could get you to talk about your shapeshifting. I don't think we want that."

"I just hate not knowing what happened during those missing hours."

Dagger grabbed the carafe and filled his cup. "I hate being drugged and I hate not knowing if I had something to do with Diego's death."

"And losing Skizzy's Cadillac."

"That, too."

"At least I didn't lose my new boots."

"I have made a clothes horse out of you. Don't you ever miss those sack dresses your grandmother made you?"

Sara smiled wistfully as memories of her youth flooded back. It had been a life of seclusion and fear. "I miss my grandmother."

They grew silent, each looking at the drive down to the front gate and the bright light from the full moon which splashed across the maple and willow trees. They had felt safe on the gated three hundred acres. But something loomed on the horizon. Sara could feel it. Dagger, on the other hand, felt it was already here.

16

Padre bent down and studied the body on the park bench. The white suit made the deceased look like a beached whale lying on its back.

They may need an oversized gurney and a couple more men just to haul the dead weight off the bench.

Luther nodded at one of his interns and together they rolled the man onto his side. The bench screeched in protest. It felt to Luther like trying to lift a sequoia tree. "No blood, nothing soiling his pretty white suit."

Padre opened the wallet Luther had retrieved from the victim's pocket. "Lotta money here." He pulled out a wad of credit cards. "Robbery was definitely not the motive."

"His Rolex is still on his wrist," Luther said as he and his assistants set the sequoia back on his back. Then he lifted one side of the jacket. "Even his gun is still in its holster."

Padre pulled out more cards. "He has a concealed carry permit and what do you know, a drivers license. Poor guy hasn't lost weight in five years. "Embuerto Gomez. There's a business card here for Gomez Imports. What fine upstanding businessman goes for a walk in the park this early in the morning?"

"More like moonlight. This guy has been dead for at least eight hours. I'd say he died between eleven and two."

"Maybe he drowned and someone moved his body to the park?" Padre did a mental estimate of the number of blocks to the nearest beach. This side of the park was isolated.

Except for a pond where ducks gathered, most of the activity occurred on the north end of the park where there were grills and volleyball nets. Large oak trees shielded this section yet could be easily accessed from a gravel road used by maintenance trucks.

"Nah. Suit isn't even wet." Luther stepped away as his men lugged the gurney, trying hard not to let the wheels touch the ground. It was difficult enough carrying the weight let alone having to drag the gurney down the dirt road. "A guy this size had to have had some health issues."

Padre stood and scratched his head. The deceased looked peaceful, as though a mortician had prepared him for the family viewing. The hands were crossed at the chest, the suit jacket straightened and buttoned. Even the damn tie knot looked flawless. A mugger wouldn't have taken the time to position the body nor would a mugger have left the money in the wallet. No, this had been personal. Someone close to Embuerto Gomez had placed his body in the park.

Padre didn't hold much hope that the forensics team had gathered anything useful. Fifty yards away behind the crime scene tape stood two crusty members of the park crew who had found the body when they arrived to pick up dead branches and debris. Padre had already called the park district office and confirmed the start time for the workers. Anyone could look at their pale faces and shaking hands and know the old codgers had been shocked by the discovery.

Padre nodded in the direction of the crime scene tape. "I don't think those two have any more to add to their statements. All I need now is a cause of death."

Luther couldn't contain his amusement as he watched his men trying to maneuver the gurney into the back of the transport van. "Probably a heart attack. The guy looked one taco away from a cardiac arrest."

* * *

Skizzy's face popped up on the computer monitor. "Yo, anyone home?"

Dagger pressed a button. "Go."

"The drug test came back. You had some designer shit in your system. Some type of a midazolam with a bit of the date rape drug maybe. My guy doesn't know exactly what. Said there's all kinds of shit over the borders. It's what they use when you go for outpatient surgery. You're actually awake, but don't remember a thing. Blocks your memory, big time."

"Make sure you tell the drug company it works very well, maybe too well. We not only don't remember anything after being drugged, but we also have a blank slate for the entire day."

"Aliens, I tell you. Who's that couple that got kidnapped decades ago and were missing twenty, thirty hours of their lives? And now these two guys missing their brains. Maybe when the mother ship tried to beam them up, something went wrong. They only got the brains and not the rest of their bodies."

Dagger tried not to laugh. It would only encourage the nutty guy. "Wait. You said two guys?"

"Yeah." Skizzy punched a few buttons and a photo popped up on Dagger's monitor. "This guy was found on a park bench earlier today. According to Padre's report, of which I will not cop to how I obtained, the deceased owned the bar where you and Sara went to find out more about that Diego fella. Vague M.E. report, just like with Diego, tells me he could be missing his brain, too." The image appeared on the screen.

Sara gasped. "It's Embuerto."

17

Padre sighed as the steno pad hit his desk. "My, my. Haven't you been a busy man." Sheila leaned over the desk giving Padre a gaze at a very nice cleavage.

"Can you get those two out of my face, please?"

"Oh, you priests have no self-control."

"And cut it with the priest jokes. There are more teachers guilty of abusing children than priests. Go harass them." Padre leaned away from the melons as Sheila faked a pout and took a seat in front of the desk.

"I understand you found a possible associate of Diego Manuel in the park this morning...dead."

"Embuerto Gomez, a fine upstanding citizen. How they connect, I don't know. I haven't been able to get a search warrant for the premises nor find anyone in the bar who will admit to even knowing Gomez. And how would you know if the two knew each other?"

Sheila flashed her runway smile. "A little bird told me Gomez is the one who put up bail for Diego a few times."

Damn. Padre hated it when the press had better sources than he had. "Maybe you should flash those melons around that bar and find out some more answers."

"Still think it's drug related?"

"Never said I did. The CPPD doesn't speculate."

"No blood at the scene, no sign of injuries on the body. Sounds like another drug overdose."

Padre congratulated himself for keeping his bored mask on and wondered what big mouth at the scene leaked information. He could vouch for his people and Luther's. Maybe the clean up crew?

"Could be his competition is lacing the product. Still gotta wait a couple weeks for the tox screen report. In the meantime…" He made a shooing motion with his hands. "Why don't you go do your investigating elsewhere. I'll share what I find out and you can do the same."

"Fat chance, my little taco. Whatever I find comes with a price."

He watched her sashay out of his office, then shook his head. The military should use her to interrogate suspects.

Padre checked his watch. A neighbor of Juanita Gomez stated that the wife went to church every morning, then went to breakfast and returned home around noon. He grabbed his trench coat and almost made it to the door when his cell phone rang. It was Luther. The medical examiner only called Padre on his personal cell phone whenever he had something critical to tell him.

"Please tell me Gomez died of a cardiac arrest."

"We have big problems."

Padre stepped into Chief John Wozniak's office, closed the door and leaned against it.

"Got answers on the Diego case?" Wozniak asked as he struggled to work sausage size fingers on pea size numbers of a calculator. When he didn't hear his sergeant reply he looked up. "What?"

"Embuerto Gomez."

"The dead guy in the park this morning?"

Padre didn't nod, didn't blink, hardly even breathed.

"Don't tell me...he didn't...he wasn't...Jesus, Mary and Joseph!"

"Even they can't help us."

"Juanita Gomez?" Padre hated talking through a screen. The woman staring back filled the doorway. A boy around five hung onto her leg, what looked like jelly smudged on his face. Padre held up his badge. She didn't seem impressed. "Could we talk for a few minutes?"

"What about?"

"Embuerto."

"I already know he's dead. Pardon me while I make party plans." She flipped a lock and said, "Come in."

Padre stepped over trucks, building blocks, and a toy train. Unopened mail and empty soda cans littered a coffee table. A television set blared in a corner where two older boys sat, one around seven and another possibly eight.

"Welcome to my world," Juanita said. She pointed to the two boys on the floor. "Take your brother and go watch TV in my bedroom. Go now."

They jumped to attention and dragged the five-year-old out of the room.

"I'd offer you coffee but I don't drink it, don't have it."

Padre wondered why a drug king lived in a house no bigger than his own. Juanita ran a hand through her thick hair and pulled it back in a ponytail. Her body had been shoved into a pair of stretch pants, and the Taste of Chicago shirt barely covered her ass.

"How did you find out about your husband?" Padre found a chair that didn't look covered in crumbs.

"Word travels. I got a phone call last night."

"We didn't find him until this morning."

Juanita took a seat on the couch and pulled her legs up under her. "Guess my grapevine works better than yours."

"Who told you? It's possible that person could have information that could help us uncover how he died."

"Number one, I say good riddance. Number two, I haven't seen him in three years. He has one of his gophers deliver a monthly allowance to me."

Padre couldn't help noticing the chipped polish on her nails. Any attempt at pampering appeared to come second to raising three boys.

"Do you work?"

"Embuerto believed a woman's place was in the home, tending to the babies. Once Julio, my youngest, started pre-school, I took a job as a bus driver. Word got back to Embuerto and I ended up with a broken ankle, the one I would use on the gas pedal."

"You didn't press charges?"

She laughed as though he didn't understand their customs. "What? And have my fingers that dial the phone broken? Besides, Embuerto never dirties his hands. He has one of his minions do it."

Padre pulled out a small notepad from his shirt pocket and opened it to a list of questions. "Did Embuerto have any health issues?"

"If you are asking if he did drugs, yes, but only to test the merchandise. If I voiced my objection to his line of work, well, I would only do it once."

"There's got to be more than drugs in a warehouse that size."

Juanita studied her chipped nails. As the silence stretched, she sighed. "I've heard they do a bit of car repairing back there."

"Car repair? Or chop shop?"

Another sigh. This time it came with one tear making a lazy trail down her puffy cheek. She may at first have seemed hard-hearted when speaking about her cheating husband, but the hurt and grief for the father of her children were clearly written on her face.

Padre examined the marred walls, worn furniture, and stained carpet. Embuerto did not die a poor man. "How is it you aren't living in a mansion, with all that money?"

The tear appeared to evaporate quickly as Juanita's face hardened. She looked around the room as though noticing for the first time that she actually lived in a dump. "He spends all of his money on himself and that tramp girlfriend of his."

Padre clicked his pen. "What's the tramp's name?"

This brought a slight smile to her face. "Carlotta Regina Ramirez. I have a broken dish washer. She has a nice set of tits bought and paid for by Embuerto, along with a tummy tuck, an ass lift, face lift, and a Mercedes convertible. He takes her on exotic vacations while I drive a beat up Chevy to Walmart."

"Do you know of any problems he has had with anyone lately?"

"Three years it's been." She held up three fingers as though he hadn't heard her the first time. Padre wondered if she were Italian instead of Hispanic or do they all talk with their hands? "I have never been privy to who he hires and fires."

"Yes, but you said you have a grapevine. I bet there is someone on your husband's staff who is loyal to you, maybe didn't like how Embuerto treated you." He leaned in, his voice a whisper as she played with her hair. "Your husband can't hurt you now."

"I washed my hands of the whole business. Even when I married Embuerto I told him, 'Don't you bring your business home. I don't want my kids exposed to your shit.' And he didn't."

Padre gave those words a few seconds to sink in. The men would have been loyal to Embuerto, but what about the women? Would Juanita chance word getting back to her husband? After all, one cat fight and loyalties turn.

"Whoever is in your grapevine, did she ever mention any new designer drugs your husband had been distributing?"

A crash came from one of the bedrooms followed by yelling. Juanita charged from the room. "WE HAVE COMPANY. NOT ONE MORE SOUND UNTIL YOU HEAR THAT SCREEN DOOR CLOSE. HAVE I MADE MYSELF CLEAR?" She returned to the couch while a stillness settled over the house. Padre slowly sat up a little straighter. "Where was I? Of course, that shit Embuerto peddled. No, I have not heard of anything new. Embuerto was making tons of money with the drugs. He didn't like meth. Too messy and dangerous. Cocaine, pills and, yes, the chop shop."

Padre jotted it down in his notepad. A new wrinkle in the case. Too bad he couldn't get a warrant to search the warehouse. How clever of Embuerto's people to dump the body far from the warehouse.

"You didn't hear it from me." Her eyes crawled around the room, seeming to examine every crack in the ceiling and rip in the carpeting. "Maybe his life insurance money can get us out of this hell hole." As though realizing how calloused that sounded, she exposed a more concerned look and asked, "How did he die? He didn't commit suicide, did he? Would be just my luck. I wouldn't get any insurance money."

So much for hiding a calloused exterior. "Are you aware of any health conditions, maybe a congenital heart defect? Diabetes? We haven't found a visible cause of death yet, so poison certainly isn't out of the question. You certainly sound like you would have had an axe to grind."

"Believe me. If I wanted to kill my husband, I wouldn't have stopped at him. I would've gotten the bitch, too."

18

"Carlotta Regina Ramirez," Padre said to himself as he typed the name into his dashboard computer. "Whoa, hottie." He could understand why Juanita would be envious. It only proved that money could buy you just about any woman you wanted. Embuerto obviously lavished his honey with all kinds of gifts and toys while Juanita had to keep the home hearth and his kids that he never saw. What woman wouldn't want to put a bullet between his eyes? But that wasn't how Embuerto died. According to Juanita, Embuerto and Carlotta were inseparable so she had to have seen something last night and would know who moved the body.

He had called Dagger after leaving the widow's house to ask if he had a second brain lying around anywhere. Padre had hoped Dagger had dug up information on some new drug sifting through the Midwest. So far Dagger had come up empty. If a criminal could outwit Chase Dagger, the city was in deep shit.

Padre punched several keys and put out a BOLO on Carlotta, should she be headed for the airport. The BOLO also stated the make and model of her Mercedes as well as Embuerto's vehicles, should she have access to them.

Padre kept the last known home address on his screen and made a U-turn, heading to one of the few gated communities in Cedar Point. He showed his badge to the security guard at the gate and asked if he had seen Carlotta Ramirez lately.

He wasn't much help since he had just come on duty. "I'd appreciate it if you'd call whomever you replaced, ask him the same question, and call me at this number." Padre handed him a business card. "What about Embuerto Gomez? I believe he lives with her." Another head shake told Padre that Embuerto paid people a lot of money to keep quiet. As he drove on through to Carlotta's house, he hoped the guard didn't call to give her advance notice.

"Sweet, Jesus." Padre let out a long whistle as he passed brick driveways and massive structures with wrap-around flagstone decks, in-ground pools, and multiple terraces. "So this is how the other half lives. I have got to go into the drug business." He punched another button and let the GPS find the address. He didn't want to waste time wandering a large community giving Carlotta more time to pack a bag and head out of town, if she wasn't already halfway to Florida.

You have reached your destination, the robotic voice said.

The brick drive led to a five-car garage, its doors closed. He could see shutters on the windows on the first and second floors. He parked his rusted sedan in the circular drive and made his way up the steps. This gated community may be high end, but the residents had a way to go to match Robert Tyler's wealth. The Tylers were one of the richest families in Cedar Point. The wealthy could afford just about anything they wanted. Except for young Nick Tyler, who had been dating Sara off and on. He had even presented her with an engagement ring which Sara had declined. One of the most sought after bachelors in the country and Sara turned him down. Padre didn't have to think hard to figure out why.

Robert Tyler's wealth was equal to Leyton and Anna Monroe's, Sheila's parents. Their homes overlooked Lake Michigan. Sheila wouldn't be caught dead living in a gated community. She had once said they were gated prisons with homes built on top of each other and neighbors who resembled Stepford wives.

Padre wondered if Juanita ever found her way into this gated community to find out how her husband lived. By keeping the house in Carlotta's name, his enemies wouldn't be able to find him. But if Padre could, anyone could.

He pressed the doorbell and heard a saintly cathedral chime. Almost crossed himself. It brought back memories of his days in the seminary. He and Chief Wozniak had attended the same seminary. However, John had found women too tempting, and Padre would rather protect people than preach to them.

He pressed the doorbell again.

"Ain't nobody home." An elderly man next door stopped clipping offshoots from what looked like a lilac bush. He set his clippers down and shuffled over.

Padre showed his badge. "Detective Sergeant Jerry Martinez with CPPD. What is your name, sir?"

"Now you come. Where were you when they had all their drug parties with bands playing that loud *maca-hootchie* music by the pool til four in the morning?"

"I would have come and shot them all, sir." Padre hoped he could take a joke.

"Donney Campbell, Sergeant." A straw hat blocked the sun from a skin lined with age. Clippings clung to his quilted flannel shirt and worn jeans.

Padre hadn't expected someone rich enough to live in this community to still do his own yard work. "When is the last time you saw the owner?"

"Lots of people coming and going. The man, boyfriend I think. Haven't seen him since yesterday. They both left together around two in the afternoon. Always coming in at four in the morning, then sleeping late, or lounging at the pool hungover. She came back around midnight with a different guy, younger. They were yelling about a demodo or something like that."

"*Demonio*? That means demon," Padre offered.

"She said something about, 'go take care of it.' Then he took off."

"You must stay up late."

"I sleep off and on. Slightest noise wakes me. What I'd give for an uninterrupted eight hours of sleep."

"Have you tried sleeping pills?"

"And miss all the fun?" He cackled, then broke into a coughing fit. "Someone once said sleep was nothing more than little slices of death. Guess I just want to see the grim reaper when he comes."

"Did you get a look at the guy?"

"Nah. Too dark. Sounded like a young fella, and he was skinny so it wasn't that Embuerto guy. I think she called him Socks, or something like that. Could have been something in Spanish. Thought she was calling for her dog or cat, not that she owns one."

"Did he ever come back?"

"About three or four hours later. Then she backed her car out of the garage and had him load what looked like suitcases into the trunk. He took off and then she did, too. Hope to God they are gone for good. Can't stand the partying and drugs. Gives the neighborhood a bad reputation."

Padre handed him a business card. "If you think of anything else or if you see anyone returning to this house no matter the time of day or night, give me a call."

"Sure thing."

Padre loved neighbors, especially the elderly ones. They see and hear just about everything. Padre wrote down

Donney's number should he have any additional questions in the future.

19

"Can you tell where it took place?" The hand with the Jaeger-Lecoultre watch rested lightly on the shoulder of his trusted assistant. Fredrik adjusted his glasses then minimized the video exhibiting another example of a death by mysterious means. The victim looked Hispanic and dressed like a gang banger. The video replayed while Fredrik completed a search and Keyes timed the death on his watch. "Amazing how he has reduced the kill time practically in half." His expert eyes studied the scene closely looking for any telltale sign of where the murder had taken place.

"This doesn't look like the desert or an isolated place where he could dispose of the body," Fredrik noticed. "He couldn't possibly have killed this man where there could be witnesses or police involvement. Could he be that stupid?"

Keyes straightened, his face showing controlled incense. He walked to the window and looked out on the white capped North Shore Mountains. City lights flickered below as he watched a dinner cruise ship sail toward Coal Harbor. "Search the license plate of the vehicle and see if it appears on any police reports."

Fredrik enlarged the video again, then zoomed in on the license plate. "I'll start with the United States, sir. The plate is from Michigan."

Keyes braced himself on the patio door, cursing his decision to work with Mason Godfrey, a man who did not know the meaning of the word discretion. Godfrey flaunted his wealth and had one major distressing flaw—he enjoyed taking chances.

"I found it, Sir." Fredrik looked up from the keyboard. "I cross-checked the license plate number of the vehicle with any open police reports throughout the United States." He vacated the seat and turned it so his boss could sit down. Fredrik's movements seemed almost mechanical. He could anticipate his boss's needs and concerns as though he could read his mind, and he knew his boss trusted him implicitly. "The death is an open police report in Cedar Point, Indiana."

"Cedar Point?" Keyes did a quick search and brought up a map. "It's about thirty miles from Chicago." He checked the cities surrounding the town. "The idiot! Now it's an open police report which will bring unwanted attention."

"Shall I tell your pilot to file a flight plan for O'Hare Airport?"

The search arrow on the map moved up and slightly to the east. "No. Let's make it Gary, Indiana, and have the pilot arrange for a helicopter."

20

Sara barely had her morning cup of tea when she heard drawers slamming. She found Dagger in his office cubical kicking the bottom filing cabinet drawer shut. Sara frowned at the papers scattered around the living room. "We've been through all of your files twice already. This is wasted energy. We should be looking for this Preacher guy." Sara took a seat on the rug, her back against the couch.

"Aren't you bothered that someone got that close to us to drug us and leave us in a damn cemetery?" Dagger ripped papers into bits and tossed them on the floor. The litter dared to float onto the large area rug. Sara glared at him and he could feel the ice blues tearing into him. "I'll clean it up."

"You better." Sara and her grandmother had sparsely decorated with used furniture and thrift store accessories. When Sara had accumulated three months' salary and rent from Dagger, she had studied decorating magazines and visited endless stores. Dagger's penchant for everything black, gray and chrome didn't meld well with Sara's need for color. She loved flowers and various shades of pink. Her pride and joy was the area rug in shades of mauve, rose and cream. Even the Florida room carried the floral theme. Some days Dagger felt like his eyes were bleeding from all the color.

Dagger started picking up the scraps of paper.

"Why do you keep old newspapers and magazines? They

aren't even addressed to you." Sara held up a *Soldier of Fortune* magazine addressed to Simon.

"Research material."

"And *Science Today* magazine stolen, I see, from the local library."

Dagger crossed his legs at the ankles then plopped down on the rug. "Just want to see the latest inventions."

"You still don't know what Sheila's up to, do you?"

"Nope, and I don't care."

"I think Sheila is going to show that photo to Padre or her boyfriend, not directly. Not her style. She'll leave the photo lying around her desk when her boyfriend stops by or have it accidentally fall out of her purse when she's in Padre's office."

"I don't think so. Sheila's style is to blackmail me to spend the night with her or go back with her altogether. She'll have that photo and multiple copies sitting in a safety deposit box somewhere until the case is solved and she no longer has any leverage."

"You haven't given any more thought to Padre's case either," Sara pointed out.

"I can't help him if I don't know anything. My main concern is my missing day."

"Have the satellites moved at all?"

"No, and I'm beginning to think the screen is frozen in place, not showing me the changes."

So now he suspects good news, Sara thought. She moved from her comfortable spot and started picking up the ripped pieces of paper. "We should go talk to the warden. Maybe he's heard of this Preacher."

The sound of bubbles floated from the computer. Dagger clamored from the floor and pressed a computer key. "Found my Caddy, Skizzy?"

"You mean my Caddy? Sure, I found it. It's still in the impound."

"You know what I mean. You were checking the camera feeds in the area."

"Just get your ass over here." The call ended abruptly.

"Well, well. If it isn't our coffin duo back from the dead." Simon straightened from his post behind the counter, his elbow on the morning paper.

Dagger gave Simon a death ray stare as Skizzy slammed seven dead bolts home and turned the *Open* sign to *Closed*. "Don't you ever work?"

"Short day, plus it's a three day work week for me. I've got seniority." Simon tapped the newspaper. "See they got another body."

"Padre's getting a bit anxious. He wants me to check Skizzy's refrigerator for brains."

"Funny." Skizzy scampered behind the counter and reclaimed his laptop.

"What have you found?" Dagger pulled a stool over and took a seat.

"Galldangmotherfuckinsonsofbitches." Skizzy stared at something non-existent on one of the shelves while Simon rolled his eyes.

"Who are you talking about?" Sara asked.

"Aliens, government, terrorists, you name it." Skizzy dragged a hand across his stained camo shirt while his eyes checked again to see if all of the locks had been bolted on the door.

Simon grabbed a carafe from a side burner and helped himself to a cup of coffee. He took a sip of the thick brew and winced. "Gee whiz, what the hell did you make this out of? Squeeze your dirty socks into a pot of water?"

Skizzy sneered at the portly postman. "Keeps people from helping themselves to my coffee. It tasted better fresh. That pot is three days old."

"Damn, I can't drink this shit." Simon walked around the curtain to the back room to spill the coffee into the sink. He returned and planted himself on a stool next to Skizzy.

Skizzy pounded away on the keyboard. "Good stuff on a few of the cameras I've been able to hack into. Big Brother is always watching, remember that."

"There." Dagger pointed at the parking lot across from the restaurant. "We don't look drugged there." On the monitor Dagger and Sara were climbing into a white limousine. "Had to be something we drank in the limo."

"What about your Cadillac, Skizzy?" Sara asked. "Any of the cameras show it being stolen?"

"Nope. Can't tell where he parked it."

Dagger mentioned how Sheila had taken a picture of him in the Cadillac and he had been headed north, probably in the direction of the hotel.

"Sheeeit. Is the rich bitch stalking you now?"

"Wouldn't put it past her," Simon added.

"She'll use it for blackmail." Dagger braced his arms on the glass showcase which contained antique jewelry, watches, and knives. He patted his pocket, then remembered he had left the slip of paper on his dresser. He had wanted Skizzy to check the numbers he had been dreaming. "If Padre ever sees the photo Sheila has, I'm going to be his number one suspect."

Simon scoffed at that. "Hate to tell you, but if Sheila was able to snap your picture driving the Cadillac, you bet your sweet ass Padre got some spy camera in town with your mug all over it."

Skizzy retrieved a box from under the counter and placed it in front of Dagger. "Got that new toy of yours finished." He used tweezers to carefully lift a tiny insect from the box.

"What the hell?" Simon leaned closer and almost bumped heads with Sara. "Is that a mosquito?"

"Yep." Skizzy placed it in the palm of Dagger's hand.

"Have any problems adding the tracking technology?" Dagger held it up for closer inspection.

"Is that another drone?" Sara remembered the remote spiders Dagger and Skizzy had developed which had been equipped with audio and visual surveillance. The mosquito had translucent wings; and except for the black dashes on the legs and body, it looked authentic.

"Got the technology right off the government web site." Skizzy beamed like a new father. "It's remote control, has a camera, microphone." He pointed to the mouth of the insect where a tiny wire protruded. "That there is a tracking device. The drone can implant it on anyone you want."

Simon rubbed a hand across the stubble on his face. It was always a losing battle trying to keep Dagger on the straight and narrow. And the depth of Dagger's knowledge about all things unusual and ahead of its time amazed him. "Where do you plan on using this thing?"

Dagger held his hand out and Skizzy carefully removed it. He turned his dark eyes on Simon and said, "An opportunity always presents itself."

Skizzy grabbed a zippered pouch from under the counter and set it in front of Sara. "Got something for you."

"For me?" Sara watched as he unzipped a section on the front of the case and withdrew several small buttons with tiny antenna on each. Then he unzipped the case itself and pulled out a flat black screen, no larger than a hand-held GPS. He held up one of the buttons. "If you see anyone suspicious, you just put one of these here puppies onto a car. It's magnetic so it won't fall off. Then you turn this baby on." Skizzy pressed a button and the screen lit up. "Just press the screen at the top to zoom in or pull back. See this tiny red blip on the map? Shows you where the tracker is. Simple."

"Thanks, Skizzy." Trackers weren't foreign to Sara. The diamond stud earring near the top of her left ear had been given to her by Dagger. It contained a tracking device so Dagger could locate her if she were ever injured in one of her shifted forms.

"Nothing for me?"

Skizzy studied Simon for a few seconds. "How about a fresh pot of coffee?"

21

"Missus Gomez." Sheila pounded harder. She knew someone was home because she had heard kids fighting. No woman would leave kids home alone. "Missus Gomez. I'm Sheila Monroe with the *Daily Herald*. Could I ask you a few questions about your husband?"

"Go away. I have nothing to say to you people," came a yell from the other side of the door.

Sheila's gaze ran from her tailored jacket to her feet. It probably wasn't a good idea to wear Manolo shoes and a Prada jacket in this neighborhood. She glanced at her gold Jag sitting at the curb. Two suspicious guys had emerged from the house across the street and had their sights on the Jaguar.

"I only have a few questions."

The front door opened a crack. A round face and dark eyes filled with hate stared back at her. "Go ask that whore of a girlfriend of his. Now beat it before I call the cops." The door slammed shut, rattling the screens on the window.

"Great." Sheila turned and headed toward the curb. The two hoods from across the street were leaning against her car, caressing the bumpers. She reached into her shoulder bag as she approached. One thing about a Monroe—they never backed down from a fight and never showed fear. Leyton Monroe believed if you couldn't threaten them with the power of your glare, then you bribe them.

In her left hand, Sheila flashed her press badge. In her right hand she held up a wad of hundred dollar bills. "Feels nice, doesn't it?" She nodded at the gleaming car.

"Like the smooth skin of a well-rounded ass," one man with a gold tooth said in broken English. Then his eyes saw the greenbacks in her hand.

"What can you tell me about Embuerto Gomez? And don't say he's dead. Tell me what I don't know." Sheila shoved her press badge back into her purse, then fanned the hundred dollar bills onto the hood of her car. "Don't worry. I'll be sure to state 'anonymous sources' so you won't get into any trouble." She could see the wheels rolling in their heads and the dollar signs in their eyes. Both boys didn't look old enough to vote, and she wondered why they weren't in school. The older of the two had strange symbols tattooed on each arm. It was an amateur job and she almost asked if a toddler scribbled on his arms. When their eyes roamed to several vacant homes on the block that would be a prime place to lure her, immediately the Monroe edict of *show no fear* reared its bright, shiny head. "Don't even think about it," Sheila warned. "I can have ten squad cars here in two minutes. Just be thankful you can make some easy money today."

Tats Incorporated was the first to mention a certain girlfriend by the name of Carlotta. And since news traveled fast, he already knew she had been hauled into police headquarters.

"Carlotta Regina Ramirez." Padre dropped the file folder on the table and plopped in a chair across from Embuerto's main squeeze. "Your picture does you no justice." He smiled all friendly like, seeing if she was the type to save her own ass. All she did was cross her arms under her huge breasts and stare at the wall behind him.

"Word is, where Embuerto goes, you go. Which tells me you were with him around midnight when he died. Want to tell me what happened?"

She scooted her chair out, crossed her legs, then studied something on the wall by the door. So, she wasn't a snitch, but how much self-preservation did she have?

"You were the last person to see him alive. Maybe you found out he changed his will to leave everything to his wife." Padre tossed out the bait to see if the fish nibbled.

"What do I care. The house is in my name. It's an admirable father who sees that his children are taken care of."

Huh? If Padre wasn't mistaken, he'd swear Carlotta actually cared for the guy. He pulled bifocals from his pocket and put them on.

"Was Socks with you last night when Embuerto died?"

"Who? You mean Socko?"

Padre had checked with the gang task force files to find out Embuerto's known accomplices. Such lists don't always include the strange nicknames they give each other. "Do you know his real name?"

Carlotta waved a hand which rattled the numerous bracelets circling her wrist. "Sokoloski, or something like that."

Padre stared over the tops of the bifocals. "He's Polish?"

"His father, I think."

Padre consulted the list again. "Sammy Sokoloski. That must have been hard to relate." His guest continued searching for something more interesting to examine on the walls and ceiling. "Did he and Embuerto have an argument?"

She flicked her eyes back to Padre, possibly tiring of

whatever she had been staring at. "Socko was the little brother Embuerto never had."

"And Diego? He must have pissed off someone to end up in the trunk of a car."

Carlotta studied him for the longest time. He saw intelligence behind those eyes. For all of her fake lashes, boobs, and ass, there were lights on in the tower. "How did Diego die?"

"You tell me. Maybe one of his people used poison."

"Poison?" She straightened and turned in her chair to face him. "That means it would have to be someone he knew, someone he trusted." Padre nodded as she spoke, then Carlotta gasped. "You think it was me? I loved him. I would never hurt him."

"Then tell me what happened." Padre had all the time in the world. Uniformed officers had already tracked down Socko. He hadn't driven far before state troopers pulled him over on I-65 for a DUI. He had spent the night in the drunk tank before being delivered to the precinct. Padre could see her weighing her options. "Is this some gang turf war? We can put you in protective custody."

Carlotta shook her head and tears started pooling in her eyes. It wasn't sadness or remorse Padre saw. It was fear. "I don't know what happened. One minute Embuerto was standing there talking to us, the next minute he fell to the ground, his body jerking like…like a seizure or something."

"He must have done something before that. Did he choke, grab his chest, gasp, look like he was in pain?"

"*Nada.* Nothing like that. He just keeled over, but it was his eyes. How weird."

Padre looked up from his notes. If Carlotta could shed some light on what happened to Embuerto, it would help to explain what happened to Diego.

"What about his eyes?"

"Socko and me. We thought Embuerto had a stroke or a heart attack. Then when he fell…" She wrapped her arms around her body and shivered. "So strange. You know how it looks when steam comes off of hot ice? That's how it was. This narrow puff of steam came out of Embuerto's nose, ears, and the pupils of his eyes. Oh my God. What could have happened?"

22

Padre set a cup of hot coffee in front of Carlotta. Her hands shook as she reached for the cup. Whatever happened last night, whatever Carlotta witnessed, it scared her to death.

"What did you do after Embuerto fell?"

"Got the hell out of there. Socko drove me home."

"What did you mean when you told Socko to take care of it?"

One perfectly formed eyebrow jerked up. "Has that nosy old man been talking to you? Doesn't he ever sleep?"

"Lucky for me, no."

Carlotta clammed up, preferring to study the steam rising from the cup. Fearful that he might have lost her cooperation, Padre said, "I don't care about Embuerto's business in the warehouse. I deal in homicides, and until my medical examiner can prove Embuerto died of natural causes, I have to assume he died of unnatural causes. You wouldn't want to see his killer go unpunished, would you?"

She took a swipe at her eyes, not caring if her makeup smeared. "I thought they should move the body so police wouldn't have a reason to search the warehouse. Couldn't have that. So they moved him to the park."

"Did Embuerto have Diego killed?"

She was shaking her head before Padre finished the sentence. "Diego and Embuerto were tight. They had been running a scam on Preacher. Preacher, he…" She looked at the detective, her eyes like a frightened rabbit. "I've said too much already." She reached for the coffee cup and gulped down a long swallow. Padre waited. When the silence stretched, he knew she wouldn't offer anything more about this mysterious Preacher. Carlotta set the cup down and in a shaky breath asked, "What about Diego? The news didn't report how he died."

Padre chose his words carefully. "We have to wait for the tox screen, which will take a couple weeks."

Carlotta was smarter than she looked. "Did he die the same way Embuerto did?"

Padre jotted down more notes as he thought of how to respond to her question. "Embuerto had a lot of health issues. He obviously liked to eat and didn't appear to hit the gym. It takes a toll on one's health. Course, with all the designer drugs going around and given Embuerto's line of work, anyone could have laced the drugs Diego and Embuerto sampled. Anyone else have it out for Embuerto, other than the usual rival gangs? Anyone have a beef with him recently."

"No." She paused for a few seconds, then her eyes widened. "Yes!"

Padre perked up.

"This man came to see Embuerto Sunday afternoon, asking about Diego, wanting to know all kinds of things about him. Where was he last night, when did we see him last, who did he hang around with? Stuff like that. Real ballsy. Waltzed in unannounced and unarmed. Said she was his weapon."

"She?" Padre's pen hovered over the notepad. A chill slithered up his back, and dammit if his right hand didn't reach for the crucifix hanging from his neck. "Describe this couple."

"He was good looking, dark hair in a ponytail, eyes almost

black. Dark skin, more like Mediterranean. Maybe he just looked darker skinned because he was dressed all in black."

The chill slithered around to his front side.

"She was beautiful. Long hair, strangest turquoise eyes. I think she was Indian, not Hindu-type but Navaho or something. Although they don't have blue eyes, right? Anyway, Embuerto had two of his men toss blades at the guy. She steps right in front of him and grabs both knives by the handles barely an inch before they hit flesh. Then she flings them back at Embuerto and they slam into his chair, just a hair's breath from his *cojones*."

The chill now settled in Padre's *cojones* as he tried to hide his suspicions as to the identity of the couple. He remembered how Sara had saved Dagger's life during the Mitch Arnosky case. Arnosky had also flung a knife at Dagger. Sara had spun in the air, grabbed a knife from Dagger's belt while she grabbed Arnosky's knife just a hair's breath before it hit Dagger. Then she flung both knives at a fleeing Arnosky, pinning him to a tree. There was so much confusion that night that Padre hadn't taken the time to decipher everything that had happened.

Padre shook off that trip down memory lane. "They give any names?"

"No. I didn't hear them use their names. Only terms of endearment, like honey or sweetheart. Hell, even Embuerto's men would never go through such lengths to protect him. But she...she was something else." Her bracelets clanged again and she waited as though expecting Padre to have all the answers. She sat back, exhausted from reliving the ordeal. "Never met anyone before who could scare Embuerto. There was something really weird about those two."

Aw shit.

23

Padre left Carlotta in one interrogation room and walked across the hall to a second room. If Padre thought Carlotta looked scared, Socko looked ready to shed his skin and grow something camouflage in color. His eyes lowered at half-mast from a hangover while his feet and hands tapped incessantly. His eyes darted to each corner of the room and his body recoiled when Padre opened the door.

"Sammy Sokoloski. You prefer Socko, Mister Sokoloski?"

Socko blinked rapidly, then sat back, his hands finding the arms of the chair a more entertaining instrument to pound on.

Padre pulled out a chair and sat down. He set a cold can of ginger ale in front of his guest. "Good for the stomach." He used the tip of his finger to shove the can closer to the young man. "Just spoke to Carlotta. She spoke highly of you. Said you were like the little brother Embuerto never had."

The young man's hair was slicked back and wet, either from sweat or some goopy hair product. Padre could see a hint of tats peeking out from the top of a stained shirt. According to the state police, Socko had empty beer cans in the back seat of his car. Padre couldn't even drink a cup of coffee while driving without hitting a bump and wearing half of the contents down his shirt. Socko obviously had the same problem with beer and food, or Padre hoped the red stain was ketchup and not blood.

Padre nudged the can closer. "Maybe you want a couple aspirin, too?" Socko's lips pressed so close together, Padre thought he might need a crowbar to open them. "Carlotta told me she asked you to get some guys and move Embuerto's body to the park. I'm more interested in how Embuerto died. We didn't find any bullet or knife wounds so I'm thinking poison. What do you think?"

Socko stopped rocking and made a sign of the cross. "*El diablo siempre se le debe.*"

"The devil always gets his due." Although the rap sheet gave Socko's age at twenty-five, he looked and acted like a teenager. He had never finished high school and had been recruited into the gangs at the ripe young age of eleven. "Why do you think the devil had anything to do with Embuerto's death?"

"No, no. Not the devil. God. These were emissaries of God punishing us for what we do."

Padre tried for the next twenty minutes to get Socko's side of the story to see if it confirmed Carlotta's description of what had transpired. All the young man would do was mutter prayers under his breath and rock back and forth.

Chief Wozniak leaned a beefy shoulder against a wall while Padre contemplated a different line of work. The wall creaked in protest so Wozniak pulled out a chair and set his coffee cup on Padre's desk. "So we've gone from the devil killing them to God's emissaries punishing the evil."

"Oh, it gets better. Guess who God's two emissaries are?"

John wedged himself into a chair and sighed. "Am I going to like this?"

Padre handed John a photo. "A camera in a bank parking

lot happened to catch the Cadillac driving up to the light at the intersection of Baylor and Water Street."

John held the photo at arms length, then with a sigh pulled out his bifocals. He didn't spend much time on the photo before shifting his glare to his sergeant. "Have you spoken to them?"

"Not yet."

"Bring them in. Dagger has to know more about Diego. The damn Cadillac probably belonged to Dagger. He withheld information, dammit!"

"With Dagger, it's all in how you ask. He never offers. And he could hold up on that reservation property til Dooms Day and we wouldn't be able to do anything about it. Let me handle this, John."

John hefted his bulk out of the chair and tossed the photo on the desk. "He doesn't know about Embuerto Gomez yet, does he?"

"It's been in the news."

"Yeah, but he doesn't know he's missing his brain, too."

"He may." Padre folded the photo and slipped it into his jacket pocket. "If he's the one who took it."

24

Padre kicked his shoes off at the door before Sara had a chance to threaten to cut his feet off for leaving marks on her area rug.

"Beer, Padre?" Sara asked.

"Got anything stronger?" A look passed between Dagger and Sara. Padre huffed in frustration. "You guys gotta stop that."

"Stop what?" Dagger asked, all innocent like.

Padre pointed at his own eyes, then turned the finger-pointing to Dagger. "This unspoken communication you two have. It always telegraphs to me, 'what did they do now that I don't know about?'"

Dagger stepped behind the bar and poured Padre a scotch and water. Padre's unannounced visit could only mean that Sheila showed him the photo of Dagger behind the wheel of the Cadillac in whose trunk a body had been found.

Padre no sooner settled himself into the cushy loveseat then Sara set a tray with chips and dip on the coffee table along with a bowl of mixed nuts, one of Padre's favorite. He tried to push back Carlotta's comments about the mystery couple. Then his own memories of Sara in the cemetery during the Arnosky case started twitching his cop nose. He had always known her as this shy young woman who knew very little of the world outside of her grandmother's three hundred acres. Had Dagger had that big of an influence on her?

"You're spoiling me, Sara. All my basic food groups—scotch, chips, dip, nuts."

Sara's smile made her look even more beautiful, and it rustled feelings in even Padre's aging heart. He imagined sailors found the same smile on mythical sirens before they were dragged to their doom.

"You look nervous tonight, Padre." Sara grabbed a potato chip as Dagger sat down next to her on the couch and placed his beer on the coffee table.

"Weird cases. It was bad enough we had that one guy missing his brain. Now we have a second one in the morgue who met the same fate."

"Two?" Sara took another potato chip. Dagger leaned back stretching his arms across the back of the couch.

Padre had to avert his eyes from Dagger's. Carlotta was right, they were black as coal and he had a lazy blink. Padre tried not to blink for fear when he opened his eyes again it wouldn't be Sara and Dagger sitting on the couch. Instead, it would be a black panther and a siren, and Padre would be stripped of his gun and his brain.

"No sense dragging this out." Padre mustered as much authority in his voice as he could. He pulled out the photo and handed it to Dagger. Dagger didn't even look at the photo, just kept his eyes on Padre, with that same half smile that told Padre he might not leave the house all intact.

"Did you get this from Sheila?" Dagger handed the photo to Sara without looking at it.

"Sheila?" Padre shook his head. "Bank lot off the Taylor Street intersection. Same car where we found Diego's body."

"No, it's not the one Sheila had." Sara handed the photo back to Padre. They couldn't be more calm if Padre were showing them photos from his last fishing trip.

"Sheila had a photo?" Padre folded the copy and shoved

it back into his pocket.

"Yeah. I think she's stalking me. She's hanging onto it for future blackmail, I'm sure."

Padre took another sip of his scotch, sat back, and waited. And waited. Finally he cupped a hand around his left ear. "I don't hear you talking."

One knuckle found its way to Sara's mouth. For all of her transformation after working with Dagger, she still had one nervous habit that she hadn't been able to break. She used to nibble so much that her knuckles would have ugly knots on them.

Dagger reached over and gently pulled her hand away. He looked at Sara and there must have been another unspoken agreement between them because Dagger nodded ever so slightly, and Sara started to explain how they woke up in a coffin without any recollection of where they had been or whom they had seen.

Padre leaned forward as they explained searching through the house for any case file they had been working on, about their dinner at the Ritz, the hotel room where they found their clothes, and the driver who had escorted them to the white stretch limo.

After the fifteen minute dissertation, Padre set his drink down, clasped his hands and said, "You two were naked in a coffin together?"

Dagger rolled his eyes toward the ceiling. "That's it? We're kidnapped, drugged, car stolen, and all you can think of are two naked bodies? Thought you were a church going guy."

"I'm a man, I'm not dead yet. Back to the car. Where did you get the Cadillac?"

"Don't remember."

Padre took out his notepad and flipped through several

pages of notes. "That means Skizzy." He shook his head, remembering the Hummer Skizzy owned which he failed to register. How many more vehicles did the squirrelly guy own? "And you don't remember anything, not even a name?"

"No. And all of our I.D.s, weapons, even my wallet, had been left in the hotel room," Dagger explained. "According to the waitress we walked out of the restaurant of our own accord. I think whatever we drank in the limo had the drugs in it."

"And you don't remember where you parked the Cadillac? If you left it where we found it?"

Dagger shook his head. "Blank slate. And I don't like it one damn bit."

"You never met Diego before?"

"No," they replied in unison.

"What about Embuerto Gomez?"

"Never heard of him." Dagger took a long pull from his beer bottle.

Sara cocked her head and studied Padre as though he were some unique specimen she had found out in the acreage. "He knows, Dagger. Did Carlotta tell you?"

"Why lie about it?"

Dagger set the beer bottle down and rested his forearms on his knees. "Until I figure out where all the pieces go, I didn't want to say anything. It's my problem."

"But now two people are dead, and it's my problem."

"We had nothing to do with those deaths. I followed the bread crumbs. Found out Diego works for Embuerto. Thought the drug king could tell me how I connected to Diego which could tell me who placed him in the trunk and who drugged us."

"Your client must have called you to set up the meet. Did you trace the call?"

"Didn't receive a call, not even an email. I checked charges on my credit card which led me to the hotel. As far as Embuerto, he was alive when we left him."

"Barely, from what Carlotta says." He turned to Sara. "You almost cut off his crown jewels."

"Barely got close."

"They weren't that big," Dagger added with a smile.

Padre nibbled on the chips while he filled them in on Carlotta's explanation of how Embuerto died. "I don't know if she was seeing things, if maybe it was humid out, although it isn't this time of year. Seeing the vapor oozing from Embuerto's orifices scared the hell out of them."

Sara grabbed Padre's glass to refill it. "What does Luther say?" she called out from behind the bar.

"Same as Diego. No brain. No brain matter or any residue in the nose. No puncture wounds or any indication how the brain was removed."

Sara set the glass of scotch and water on the coaster and sat back down. "If it weren't for the fact that Diego was found in the truck of the Cadillac, I'd say it doesn't concern us. All we're trying to do is find a connection, but we aren't having any luck."

"Any idea who drugged you?"

"No, and the lab hasn't seen anything like it," Dagger replied.

"I could have our lab take a look."

"Sorry. If my contact couldn't label it, I doubt yours could."

Padre took a long gulp of his drink and hoped they didn't notice his hand shake. He was getting too old for these weird cases. "Before you ask, I don't know if there are any similar cases anywhere because I don't want to put it out there that we have bodies missing their brains. So far I've been able to keep details out of the press. Luther didn't even mention it in his reports." He remembered something else Carlotta had mentioned. "Have you heard of someone named Preacher?"

"Has a scar in the shape of a cross on his forehead. Embuerto mentioned him, but didn't know where we could find him," Dagger offered. "When we were in the warehouse we smelled grease, oil, gas. Caught a glimpse of auto parts in the back when the drapes parted. And since Diego jacked cars…"

"Chop shop." Padre slipped the notepad back into his pocket. He downed the last of his drink in one swallow as he thought about car parts, body parts, and drugs. He eyed the two and envied their calm demeanor while everything crumbled around him, along with his career. He sighed and slapped his hands on his thighs as he rose from the loveseat. "Guess I should go scrounge up a couple brains, since you two have nothing more to offer."

"If we did, you know you'd be the first one we'd tell," Dagger said.

"Right." Somehow Padre didn't find that comforting.

25

"Hi, lover boy. Want some pillow talk?"

Dagger knew he shouldn't have answered the phone. He propped himself up on one elbow and stared at the clock. "It's almost midnight, Sheila. I need my beauty sleep."

"Not so fast, Chase Dagger. I thought you'd like to stop by and read the police reports."

"Attach them to an email."

She laughed a light, seductive laugh saved for such occasions, like flirting or screwing someone over. "You do remember that little photo of you I have. You wouldn't want a certain someone to find it on his desk."

"No need. He has a photo of his own."

Silence. Dagger could feel the panic with each of Sheila's inhales.

"Photo?" She sounded nervous. "What do you mean he has his own?"

"He knows everything. He was over earlier and we talked about it."

More silence. If Dagger pulled the phone away he was sure he would see smoke coming from it.

"Are you fucking with me?"

Dagger laughed. "All that money spent on finishing schools and you still have a potty mouth."

"I bet Padre doesn't plan to put it in the paper the way I could."

Sheila still had that ace in the hole and Dagger didn't doubt for one minute that she'd do it.

"Go ahead. According to Padre, Embuerto had a chop shop in that warehouse. Diego jacked the Cadillac from the hotel parking lot. So your blackmail scheme isn't going anywhere." Dagger hung up and fell back against the pillows wondering how Joe Spagnola put up with her. Images of a tight coffin, flesh pressed against flesh, and satin sheets prevented his brain from shutting off. He tried to focus on the Ritz Hotel and a stretch limousine. Instead, a strange set of numbers kept floating in front of his eyes.

26

"You have a brainstorm yet on how to check for similar brain snatches without alerting the media?" Chief Wozniak dropped into a chair in front of Padre's desk. He moved a pen holder to one side and placed a quart-size coffee cup on the desk. He needed at least a quart of caffeine to start the day.

"Don't I wish. The amount of time it takes me to press the SEND button on my query, half the reporters in the country would be parked on the front steps. Maybe these Mexican drug cartels have found a new way to kill each other."

"By sucking out their brains?"

"They are cutting off heads and leaving them for the tourists to see in Acapulco," Padre said. "Maybe the head lobbing got too messy for them so they advanced to neater and cleaner methods."

"Have to tell you, Chief Loughton isn't too happy. He heard rumor that Cedar Point is close to becoming the distribution center for drugs and human trafficking. It's close to airports, the harbor, and major expressways. We have to shut this thing down fast."

Howard Loughton was the police chief, whereas John Wozniak was the chief of detectives. If the mayor wasn't happy, he let Loughton know about it and all the way down the chain of command.

"What about your two witnesses? Socko and Carlotta? Are they buying the story that Diego and Gomez died of drug overdoses?"

"So far. They also bought the cold air/hot body vapor song and dance. Lucky for us Diego doesn't have any relatives and the widow wants Gomez cremated. Both will end up being cremated whenever their cases are wrapped up."

"And your duo?"

Padre leaned back with a sigh before filling Wozniak in on his meeting last night with Dagger and Sara. "I have refrained from calling Luther to verify the two bodies are still there. I'm afraid he'll tell me he has the two bodies on camera shuffling out of the morgue like zombies. Just spending ten minutes with Dagger has me thinking of illogical explanations. Rational police work goes right out the window when dealing with those two."

"THAT IMBECILE!" Keyes hadn't expected Mason Godfrey to be so arrogant as to display another example so soon after the last and, again, in public where this time there were witnesses.

Fredrik waited, hands hovering over the keyboard. His eyes at half-mast displayed barely a trace of the emotion his boss showed. They had arrived at the Ritz an hour ago. Keyes knew Mason was playing a high stakes game of chess. Two players already backed out after seeing the second death. Fredrik knew his boss had elevated the high stakes game to an art form. His kind, speaking of himself and Godfrey, usually kept their distance, kept themselves above the fray. However, with this much money on the line, the stakes were too high to not have a front row seat.

Keyes stripped off his suit coat, carefully hanging it on a padded hanger and taking the time to button the two buttons. The tie remained, carefully knotted, the shirt hardly creased. "Send a message." He pulled two tumblers from the bar, added ice into each glass, then filled both glasses with scotch, 1973 Auchentoshan. He preferred to travel with his own brand of refreshments and especially liked the fruity taste of Auchentoshan at six hundred dollars a bottle. Keyes set one tumbler next to the laptop, and held the other glass as he stood behind Fredrik. Fredrik could almost hear the wheels turning in his boss's head, how easily he could put himself into the mindset of the foe. "Type the following," he instructed.

There were two witnesses to the last death. Is there a benefit to your involving the authorities?

The response was immediate:

The medical examiner's report does not include any reference to the condition of the body. As I expected, the witnesses think the victim had a seizure. As far as the police, I wanted them to know that there is something out there they aren't prepared for. They are keeping the information from the media as they kept the true details from their reports.

"Reply that I would like to meet soon to see the product." He walked over to the window and admired the scene in the distance. Lake Michigan looked clean and blue from this height. However, as with people, you never knew how repulsive it was until you got close. He planned to get up close and personal with Mason Godfrey.

"And you dreamed these?" Skizzy raised one eyebrow and lowered the other. "You sure these aren't instructions downloaded from the mother ship?"

"That's what Sara thinks. I have been repeating the same numbers in my sleep since we came back from Nebraska." At the abandoned BettaTec training camp, Dagger had been engrossed by what only he could read on the monitor. Some of it explained Dagger's past and how he trained in the underground city. Others were photos and names of people unfamiliar to him.

"Class is open boys and girls." Skizzy trained wobbly eyes on them as he tapped a pencil against the paper. "Four sets of numbers, anywhere from one digit to four, separated by periods. Anyone care to go to the head of the class?" He rocked his head back and forth and the eyes wobbled with the movement. "Anyone?"

Dagger struggled to keep from wrapping his fingers around Skizzy's pencil neck. "Just spit it out."

"It's an IP address. Look at it as an interconnected grid that allows one computer to speak to another. Although…" He studied the numbers again. "Lotta single digits here. Could be a private IP address." His eyes suddenly widened. "Jeez. It could be a direct line to BettaTec!" Skizzy dropped the paper as though someone had touched a match to it. "I sure as hell ain't accessing it from my computer. Last time I tried researching BettaTec, it almost broke through my firewall trying to find out who was hacking into their system. You try it from yours."

"I already tried my computer. I get nothing."

Skizzy shoved the paper across the counter. "Can't help, won't help, best of luck, nice knowing you."

Dagger looked at the numbers which were practically burned in his memory. He folded the paper and shoved it back in his pocket. "What about someone known as Preacher? Supposedly runs the drug business in town."

"Never heard of him."

27

Cleaves Jones, a former Joliet prison warden, owned The Joint. The beer taps resembled large hypodermic needles and two of the more popular steaks were the sizzle and the high voltage. Because he understood how difficult it could be for anyone with a record to get hired, he made an effort to employ ex-cons.

"Welcome to The Joint. What can I get you to drink?" Shondra set two menus on the table. Dagger knew from his last visit that Shondra had been in and out of prison since the age of sixteen. Theft, solicitation. Shondra had elevated pickpocketing to a science. Dimples cratered her dark cheeks and her eyes smiled as though waitressing was the most exciting thing she had ever done in her life.

Dagger ordered coffee, Sara an iced tea. "Today's special is the solitary confinement. It's pastrami on dark rye, served cold and stripped of everything. Cheese, lettuce, pickle, coleslaw, fries, and anything else you want with it is extra, and only if you are on your best behavior."

They passed on the daily special. Dagger ordered a burger and Sara a Chicken Caesar salad. "If Cleaves is around, Shondra, I'd like a minute with him."

"I'll let him know, baby." Shondra retreated to the kitchen.

Dagger kept his eyes on the door, still unable to shake the feeling that they were being followed. The lunch crowd was thinning out. Cleaves had a gold mine in the place. Customers told friends about the bars that separated the booths, the waiters and bartenders in striped prison garb, and the waitresses in skimpy orange jumpsuits. He had to chuckle at the large poster labeled WARDEN behind the bar. It showed a burly guy in tattoos with an ugly scar above one eye. Few people knew that the mild mannered guy who looked more like an accountant strolling up to the booth was Warden Cleaves Jones.

"Mister Dagger and his lovely partner, Sara. To what do I owe the privilege of your visit to my fine establishment?" The warden gave a slight bow to Sara before sliding into the booth next to her.

"The food and information," Dagger replied. Shondra returned with a tray. After distributing the food she refilled Dagger's coffee cup and made a clean getaway.

"Both of which I have plenty of."

"Preacher. Ever hear of anyone by that name? Maybe he's in charge of a church in town?"

"Not a church, not a preacher." Cleaves nodded his thanks as Shondra set a hot mug of tea in front of the warden. He took his time dipping the tea bag, then set the soggy bundle in a saucer. "Larry Hardaway, aka Lorenzo Hector something-or-other has an extensive arrest record. However, in his last stint he got some type of on-line minister license and started preaching to the inmates. He turned his childhood home into a church by nailing a cross on the front of the building and painting the building white. Idiot even carved a cross on his forehead. It was suspected he was serving more than the good word in the church so when he got tipped off by someone that the authorities were going to bust him, he closed up shop and has since kept a low profile."

"What was he serving up?"

"Prescription drugs, oxy, mushrooms, weird shit. Too many addicts shaking for their next fix garnered unneeded attention. So he shut it down." He brought out a pipe and held it up. "Do you mind?"

"It's your place," Dagger said.

He held the pipe toward Sara. "Fine with me."

Cleaves lit the pipe and puffed to get it going. The image of the accountant morphed into a lecturing professor. "Damn drugs have been around forever. As far back as 5,000 B.C. the Sumerians used opium. Alcohol wasn't even brewed until around 3,500 B.C. I think the Chinese had it right. When the British started their Opium War after China declared opium illegal, the Chinese government figured it was impossible to stop the flow into the country. So they found a way to discourage their citizens from using drugs. When they found a user they dragged him out into the street and shot him in the head. That was a game-changer."

Dagger had been told that this mild-mannered guy was one mean sonofabitch. But his toughness earned him respect.

"So you don't know if this Larry guy opened up a new church?"

Cleaves shook his head. "Last word on the street is that he has a heavy backer behind him. No one knows who. Preacher drives around in a…"

"White limo?" Dagger still had his and Sara's abduction in the back of his mind.

"Black SUV. All tricked out, dark windows. Even has his own driver. Whatever business or scam he's running, it's so far under the radar that even all of my contacts," he let his gaze roam over his hired help, "haven't been able to find out anything."

Dagger thanked him for his time and Cleaves left them to their meals.

"What do you think?" Sara pushed her plate away.

Shondra refilled Dagger's coffee cup. "Can I get you anything else?" They declined.

Dagger watched as two men entered the restaurant and took a seat at the bar. "Don't look now but I think we have two admirers."

"They look familiar?" Sara asked.

"Yeah. I think they were with Embuerto when we broke up his warehouse party. Looks like they are carrying a bit of a grudge."

"You think?" Sara noticed how they kept looking their way through the mirror behind the bar.

The two men also drew the attention of Cleaves who had noticed the bulge under their jackets. Cleaves walked up behind them, draped an arm across each of their shoulders, and whispered something in their ears. The two men reluctantly left, but not before casting one last look at Dagger.

"What do you think they are up to?"

"Nothing good." Dagger signaled for Shondra to bring the bill. He pulled a twenty and a ten from his wallet and told Shondra to keep the change.

They made their way to the door and out into the open. He had parked the Navigator around the corner and down the block. They stopped at the corner and waited to see if their two friends were lurking around a doorway or sign post. They waited another minute, then continued down the street to the Navigator.

"Maybe you were wrong. Maybe it was just a coincidence." Sara reassessed her conclusion when she noticed the Navigator sitting unusually low at the curb. And it wasn't just one side. The entire vehicle appeared to be sitting on its rims. "Or not," Sara added.

Dagger slowly circled the vehicle. "Those bastards

flattened all four of my tires."

Sara checked the sidewalk and street for any witnesses and especially the two suspicious characters from the bar. "It couldn't have been them, could it?"

"They are at the top of my list," Dagger growled. He pulled out his phone and called Skizzy.

A familiar face emerged from the drug store at the corner. She shielded her eyes, then recognition set in. The portly black woman made her way down the sidewalk waving at Sara. Her gray hair crowned her head in tight curls. She wore comfortable shoes; and although she wore a trench coat to ward off the chilly air, she didn't bother to try to button it over her massive chest.

"Good Lord, child. What are you doing standing out here on the curb?" Eunie said. Simon's wife had grown particularly fond of Sara and had filled a void in the young woman's life after her grandmother died. Eunie suddenly noticed the vehicle's tires. "Oh, my. What on earth happened?"

"Someone is sending me a message." Dagger jutted his chin toward a coffee shop on the corner. "Sara, why don't you go wait in the coffee shop. I'm going to sit here until the tow truck and Skizzy show up. Skizzy will give us a ride home."

"I haven't talked to you in so long, child. I can give you a ride home, if Dagger doesn't mind." When it came to Eunie, it was tough to say no.

28

"How are you doin, darlin', after that horrible night Simon told me about. Someone drugged you?" Eunie stirred her coffee and gave a sympathetic pat to Sara's hand. They sat at a table by the window. Few people were eating, choosing instead to nurse cups of coffee while using the café's WIFI network.

"I'm fine, really. It's just unnerving not to remember anything and to think someone got close enough to do that to us. Makes you think you're vulnerable, which certainly makes Dagger edgy."

"Right. No need to make him more edgy than he already is." Eunie had the same twinkle in her eyes that Simon often displayed. They were like bookends. Same spindly legs, rotund bodies, even their chuckles had the same infectious quality to them. "Simon said you both lost your clothes, too. That must have been, umm, quite something." She started with a smile, then broke out into her patented laugh.

"Was it ever," Sara said, more to her tea cup. "I mean it was dark and very hot in the coffin."

"I bet."

"Frightening, too. We didn't know if we were buried in the ground or at the bottom of Lake Michigan."

Eunie listened calmly as Sara explained what little they did know about the hotel, the dinner, and the white limo. "What happened to the car you drove to the restaurant?"

"Stolen," Sara replied. "Someone killed the thief and dumped his body in the trunk."

"Now I understand why Dagger is eager to fill in the blanks."

"Everything about that night is puzzling. Skizzy thinks we were kidnapped by aliens who experimented on us."

Eunie laughed until tears seeped from the corners of her eyes. "I'm sorry if it appears I'm taking this lightly. Dagger must realize that if it was done by anyone who had meant him harm, he wouldn't be alive."

"That's why he suspects Simon."

"Simon? Good lord. I don't think Simon could be that creative. He does have an alibi, though. It was our bridge night." She kept stirring her coffee with the same twinkle in her eyes. "Must make it hard for you and Dagger to keep your distance."

"Not really. Everything is still businesslike. We have already forgotten about the whole ordeal. Really."

"Uh huh." Eunie could see the color slowly rising to Sara's cheeks. "Oh, almost forgot." Eunie rummaged in one of her shopping bags. "I remembered you liked those potted flowers I had. This is the time of year to plant them so I bought you a few packages of hyacinth bulbs. The blue are the most fragrant."

"Thanks, Eunie. How sweet of you." Sara reached for her purse.

"On no, sweetheart. This is my gift. You don't owe me anything."

While Eunie paid the bill at the register, Sara glanced out of the window where a black SUV had pulled up to the curb. A teen dressed in his Sunday best slid out of the front seat, slammed the door, and started for the café. The back window of the SUV rolled down and an older man yelled something at him. As the teen entered the café, Sara kept her eyes on the man in the back, the man with a cross carved on his forehead.

"I'm parked across the street," Eunie said as they exited the café.

Sara casually reached into her purse for two items. As they walked around the back of the SUV, Sara dropped her keys. When she bent down to retrieve them, she slipped one of the trackers behind the license plate of the SUV, then hurried to catch up with Eunie.

"Did you lose something, Sara?"

"Not really. I planted a bug on that SUV."

Eunie stopped in mid-stride. "What on earth for?"

"I'll fill you in. In the meantime I hope you don't have anything planned. I'd like to see where that SUV is headed." What she really wanted to do was shift and follow the SUV, but Dagger's words of caution kept nagging at her.

Eunie clicked the key fob on her Buick Enclave. The tail lights flickered. "I'm all yours."

After Sara buckled her seat belt, she pulled the GPS from her purse and turned it on. She gave Eunie the abbreviated version of Preacher and how Skizzy had given her the trackers and the GPS.

Eunie kept a safe distance away as she watched the map on the GPS screen. "That red pulsing light is the vehicle we are following?"

"Yes, so you don't have to worry about losing them." Sara sent Skizzy a text message with the license plate number and asked him to check DMV.

"You really like what you do, don't you? Working with Dagger and all?"

"Beats gardening all day. That's about all Gram and I ever did. Plant, weed, can, bake, read. Gram encouraged me to learn to use the computer. Since we didn't own one,

I would go to the library where they gave free lessons. It's great for doing research."

"Dagger bought you a laptop?"

"Yes." Sara kept her eyes on the monitor, then enlarged the map. The SUV was headed to the east side of town.

"You know that man loves you, don't you?"

Sara kept her eyes on the monitor. "Maybe like a kid sister. Nothing more."

Eunie shook her head and smiled. "You are about as clueless as that man of yours."

"Turn right at the next stop light."

"Aye, aye." Eunie knew when a subject had been shut down.

"I think you're enjoying this."

"Almost as much fun as shopping, honey." Eunie's round face lit up when she smiled. "Let me show you something." She reached into her purse, pulled out a small holster. "My little .38 special with pink grips."

"You know how to use that?"

"Sure thing. Simon and I go shooting on Sundays at that outdoor range on Paxton. In the winter we go to the indoor paintball range for fun."

"Really." Sara hadn't realized Eunie's many talents.

The landscape changed from small businesses to single family homes on five acre lots. They passed a cemetery near an intersection dominated by gas stations and a donut shop. The red blip on the screen made a left hand turn.

"Nothing out this way except abandoned warehouses. Quarry has been closed up for years," Eunie said. "What are they guilty of?"

"He may be involved in two recent deaths. He has a scar in the shape of a cross on his forehead."

"Ah. Now things are making sense."

The red blip paused on the screen. "Looks like they've stopped." Sara switched to satellite imaging and could see the SUV parked near a large building at the quarry. "Interesting. Thanks, Eunie. You can take me home now."

"Are you sure? I am armed, you know."

Sara laughed.

29

"Why does Casey call Skizzy and not you?" Sara asked.

"Few people have my number. If Casey wants to reach me, he calls Skizzy." With the Navigator at the tire store, Dagger and Sara had driven her PT Cruiser to the bar. They stood on the sidewalk studying the brick fascia on a downscale bar called The Hideaway. A number of faux bricks had fallen away over the years, kicked out like drunken patrons. An awning listed on one side, erected by Casey in an attempt to keep the west sun from shining too much light into his establishment.

Casey stopped scrubbing the bar in mid-wipe and slowly stepped back. Dagger had that effect on people. The juke box took the cue and cut off the song, *Red Solo Cup*, causing two drunks at the bar to stop their swaying and scowl at whoever intruded on their party.

When Dagger first arrived in Cedar Point a number of years ago, Casey let him rent the apartment upstairs on the cheap. When Simon cajoled Dagger into starting a detective business, he operated it out of the apartment. Great location, cheap rent. Dagger still kept the apartment and used it to meet clients rather than having clients show up on Sara's doorstep.

"Uhhh, Dagger." Casey pulled his stained tee shirt down to cover his bulging stomach. Unfortunately, there wasn't enough fabric. "Miss Sara," he said with a nod. He edged toward the end of the bar, out of hearing distance from his bleary eyed patrons. "You have that look in your eye, Dagger." He crossed his arms and they settled onto the bulge. A tattoo of barbed wire circled each flabby bicep.

"I've had a bad week." Dagger noticed new candles on the tables and a recharger on the bar. The small candles flickered like the real thing. Sara had a number of battery operated candles in her house, which prevented a curious Einstein from sticking his beak in a real candle and burning himself. "Like what you've done with the place."

Casey gave an "aw shucks" grin. "Got new blinds on the windows, candles on the tables. I wanted to get some new wide screen telleyvisions, maybe turn the place into a sports bar, but the damn cable company wants too much for the sports network."

"Thought you only watch soap operas." Dagger checked the bar before settling an elbow on the surface.

"Well, ever since Luke and Laura broke up, I don't watch *General Hospital* no more."

"Who?" Sara asked, which prompted a headshake from Casey.

"Guess that's before your time."

"I kinda like the place sparsely populated. Makes it more of an exclusive club." Truth was, Dagger had always felt the fewer people around, the fewer people wandering upstairs for a quickie or a place to sleep it off. "Maybe it's best you don't turn this place into a sports bar, Casey. You'd need a kitchen to serve them food. Bags of chips just won't keep the drunks at bay."

"I've got a galley kitchen. What's there to offering subway sandwiches or making pots of chili? I make great chili."

Sara returned her gaze to the bar and the two drunk

patrons trying not to weave off of their bar stools. How does Casey make a living? How does Skizzy make a living? Skizzy rarely kept a thirty-hour work week.

"What's up?" Dagger tried to steer the conversation back on subject. "You told Skizzy you had a message for me."

"Oh, yeah." He walked to the cash register, opened it, lifted the tray and pulled out an envelope. "This was shoved in my mail slot and laying on the floor when I opened this morning. Had your name on it. I didn't open it."

Dagger took the envelope and read his name typed across the front. He held it up to the light slicing through the grimy windows, then ran a finger under the flap and ripped it open. When he pulled out what looked like a business card, he froze. The image of a colorful betta fish had been embossed on the card.

Sara gasped.

"What is it?" Casey tried to see what had alarmed them.

Dagger turned the card over and saw the address to his upstairs apartment. "Did whoever drop this off arrive in a limo?"

"I told you, someone slipped it into my mail slot."

"What about cameras?"

Casey slowly took a step back. "You think I can afford a security system?"

Dagger worked both hands. With his left he pulled out his cell phone and punched Skizzy's number. With the right he pulled the Kimber from its holster. When Skizzy answered, Dagger barked, "I need you at Casey's and bring some party favors."

"Uh, you're not gonna shoot up my place again, are you?" Casey yelled at their backs.

30

They waited outside at the bottom of the stairs leading to the apartment. Sara remained silent, not sure what to say. Dagger, on the other hand, had a jumble of thoughts rolling around in his head. How had BettaTec found him? How did they know about the apartment? And why now? "Guess you were wrong about BettaTec assuming I was dead."

Sara didn't know what to think. After Skizzy had found the chip in Dagger's neck, they had enlisted the help of a friend, Doc Akins, to attempt to remove it. But the chip had intricate wiring and had been attached to Dagger's brain stem. So Doc Akins removed an outside casing and planned to take it to a scientist in California to evaluate. BettaTec didn't take too kindly to rogue agents. The plane Doc Akins was on blew up over a lake. The wreckage could never be found and prevented authorities from investigating what brought the plane down. Sara convinced Dagger that BettaTec probably assumed Dagger had died in the accident.

The apartment above the bar had one large picture window and a steel door facing the alley. "Who do you think is waiting up there?" Sara asked. She wondered if Dagger could be right about BettaTec having something to do with their kidnapping. But for what purpose? She could feel the tension radiating from his body.

A vehicle resembling a large shed on wheels roared down the alley. The Humvee came to an abrupt halt. Dagger expected ten Swat team members to come pouring out rather than a scrawny guy in camo pants and shirt. He could tell by the size of the satchel Skizzy carried that he had more than just a bug sweeper in his bag. In his right hand Skizzy carried a bat. Dagger didn't question what he planned to do with it. He didn't need to fill Skizzy in on anything. Just showed him the business card with the betta fish on it.

"Oh fuck!" Skizzy stumbled back against the front bumper. "You are kidding, right? Holy shit, tell me you're kidding." When he studied Dagger's unsmiling face and predatory eyes, he said, "No problem. I've got this." He brushed past and scampered up the stairs. Skizzy stopped in front of the door and frowned. "One lock? That's it? Well, hell tarnation. Why don't ya just hang a sign that says 'Help Yourself'?"

Dagger fumbled the keys out of his pocket. "I don't live here, Skizzy. There aren't any files much less anything with my name on it." He stared at the door knob for several seconds, the key in his hand. For a second he wondered if the door had been wired to explode. He couldn't even look through the window because the blinds were closed.

Skizzy pulled a gun half the size of the bat from the satchel. It had laser sighting and a magazine almost as long as the gun. "Maybe it isn't even locked," Skizzy said.

Dagger grabbed the knob, took a deep breath, and turned it. It wasn't locked.

Skizzy went to the left, Dagger straight ahead. The room had been changed. The marred and chipped wooden desk had been replaced with a sleek black oval desk. Two plush black and gray upholstered chairs had replaced the worn ones. A large area rug in black and gray geometric designs filled most of the wooden floor. The rest of the room and walls were bare.

"When did you get the new desk?" Skizzy asked when he returned from searching the bedroom and bathroom.

Sara could hear Dagger's heart racing. She used the eyesight of the hawk to search every crevice of the room as well as the desk should it be booby-trapped.

"It's not mine," Dagger said, the words catching in his throat. "Someone's obviously been here."

Skizzy held up a hand to silence him. The door to the apartment snicked closed as Dagger leaned against it. Skizzy pulled out a hand-held device and proceeded to walk around the room.

Sara made a hand signal and pointed at the floor below. Dagger gave the same signal to Skizzy, then the two of them left the apartment.

Casey dropped a keg into the cabinet below the taps. He closed the door and straightened when he saw Dagger and Sara walk in. "Again?"

"Who changed the furniture upstairs?" Dagger braced his arms against the bar, more to keep himself from leaping at the bartender.

"What furniture?"

"Upstairs. Someone did some redecorating."

"Not me and I don't have a key to the place."

"What time did you leave last night?"

"About eleven. Place was dead."

"Did you notice the envelope addressed to me before you left?"

"No."

"And you went home and didn't see anyone with a truck parked in the alley?"

"Dagger, I didn't check the alley before I left. All I did

was lock up as usual and went out the front where my car is parked. What's going on?"

"Not sure."

"Better change the locks," Casey yelled as they walked out.

31

They returned to the second floor to find Skizzy studying his scanner.

"What did you find?" Dagger didn't like the look on his face.

"Place is clean. Bedroom, which, by the way, needs more than a college dorm futon if you ask me. The bath, this room, the closet. All clean." He turned and studied the sleek black desk. "Everything except this baby."

Sara knelt down to look under the desk. "It's bugged?" she asked.

"No bugs. Just a lot of power being generated. Don't know how. There aren't any wires, cords, nothing." Skizzy opened the top desk drawer. "And I checked all the drawers and the chairs. Nothing. Have no idea where the source is."

Dagger pulled out the leather chair and sat down. All fifty inches of the desk gleamed. It was narrow with one top desk drawer. An indent, no larger than a thumb, had been carved on the top of the desk. "What on earth is that for?"

"Looks like what them new cars have," Skizzy said. "You know, the ones you don't need a key to start? Just your thumb print."

Dagger's gaze ran along the wall, as though expecting to see a camera. His thumb hovered over the indent.

Skizzy grabbed his arm. "Wait. What if we blow up?"

Dagger put his arm down. "You're right. Maybe you two should go outside."

"Please. If they were this close to us, they could have shot us yesterday," Sara said.

Dagger hesitated, his mind racing to figure out how his location had been discovered. "They must have tracked us from Nebraska. That's the only explanation."

"Just give them your thumbprint and see what happens," Sara coaxed.

After several seconds, he pressed his thumb into the indentation. Two things happened simultaneously. A typing tray containing a virtual keyboard jutted from the underside of the desk. The keyboard glowed and appeared to be imbedded in the wood. A square section in the middle of the desktop unfolded revealing a monitor. Dagger hadn't seen any breaks or lines in the desktop to even hint at the monitor's existence.

A cursor light blinked in the upper left hand side of the screen. "Now what?" Dagger asked no one in particular.

"You need an IP address. Gotta be those numbers you showed me," Skizzy said. "Did you bring that piece of paper?"

"Didn't have to. I memorized them."

"Well, type them in. Don't just sit there like a bump on a log."

Dagger's hands hovered over the keyboard, then he moved them away. He felt Sara's hand on his shoulder.

"Doesn't matter now. May as well find out what all of this is about."

"I still think you two should leave."

"Just type already," they said in unison.

Dagger placed his hands on the keys and typed in the numbers. His finger hovered over the ENTER key for several seconds until he mustered the courage to tap it.

The screen went black, the cursor disappeared, and then words appeared on the screen.

Hello, 617. Glad you are safe.

"Shit," Dagger muttered under his breath. It was the same number they had seen on the computer screen in Nebraska. Dagger didn't know his name, only his number. He had plucked the name, Chase Dagger, out of the air and still had no idea if he had an actual name.

Skizzy cautiously stepped to the window, sure there had to be a mother ship lurking behind a cloud.

Dagger typed:

Connie?

Konrad had been the name of the network of computers that oversaw BettaTec's operation.

Connie Number Two. Please press the SPK button.

Dagger checked the keyboard and found a blue key on the top right hand side of the keyboard. He hesitated, finger over the key. He turned to his friend. "Skizzy, why don't you go down to Bill's Hardware and pick up a dead bolt for that door. Sara, you go with him."

"I think I should stay."

He slowly turned his head her way and stared, not saying anything. He waited until they left, then turned his attention back to the desk and pressed the SPK key. A mechanical voice, like what one would hear from their automobile GPS, replied. He could now communicate orally.

"*This is better, six-one-seven. We thought you died in the facility.*"

"We?" Dagger asked.

"Not important. Glad you are safe."

"How did you find me?"

"Not important."

"It is to me. I escaped your prison years ago. I have nothing more to do with you." The cursor blinked, and Dagger imagined a room of people in a bunker somewhere watching him.

"It wasn't a prison and you didn't escape. We let you leave."

"Fuckin' arrogant bastards," Dagger said under his breath. He felt his hands ball into fists as he moved away from the desk. To keep from shoving the chair across the room he crossed his arms tightly across his chest.

"We need you," the woman's monotone voice said. *"You were our best."*

"You manipulate people and control their lives. If I were to help anyone it would be to help destroy you."

"We serve a purpose."

"From the looks of those two Demkos you sent into town and that army you had in Nebraska, I'd say you don't need anyone's help."

"*Not ours.*"

Dagger laughed as he sat down, hearing the plush leather hiss. "You did hear my earlier comment about manipulation? I'm not buying it. Next you'll tell me you didn't blow that plane out of the sky or the ranger station in your quest to locate and kill me."

"*Not me.*"

Dagger let out a long breath and washed his hands over his face. "Right. I forgot. You have an internal war for power going on at BettaTec and you are on the side of righteousness."

Silence stretched for almost a full minute. Instead of a bunker, now Dagger envisioned a boardroom of ten or twelve people conferring about their next move. Suddenly an image appeared on the screen. There were several cinderblock buildings in a remote area surrounded by sand and mountains. Whoever was taking the video zoomed in on a husky man fastened to a chair with duct tape. He wore horn-rimmed glasses and had thinning hair. His panicked eyes looked huge behind the glasses as he struggled frantically against the restraints. The audio had been muted since Dagger didn't hear voices much less the sound of gun shots. All he saw was the man's eyes frozen in shock, then the body became slack against the restraints.

"What am I looking at? This a lesson to show me what happens to deserters?"

"*The dead man is Keith Barent Johnson, one of the top engineers at Rakon Industries reported kidnapped six months ago.*"

"What was he working on?"

"That's just it. Rakon Industries manufactures toys. We have found nothing in his background to suggest Johnson was working on anything clandestine."

"What does this have to do with me? It looks like the murder took place in a desert, probably the States since I don't see any camels."

"Nevada."

Dagger wasn't getting the answers he wanted. How had BettaTec found him? How long had they known he was here? If they let him leave, as they claim, then they must have been watching him all these years. For what purpose?

"I still don't understand what you want from me. You have a number of murdering clones at your disposal."

"Not a field agent of your caliber. We believe the man responsible for the scientist's death is in your area."

Dagger pushed back from the desk and paced a tight circle behind the chair. Connie wasn't offering up any helpful information yet they wanted him to go on a hunting expedition. "You want my help? Not until you answer my questions. I want to know how long you have known that I'm in Cedar Point, why did you have the Demko clones try to kill me, what is your end game here because I never know what is truth and what is bullshit when it comes to BettaTec. I find it hard to believe, with your resources, that you can't find this information on your own."

"We are a small splinter group. It's hard to know who to trust."

"I know the feeling." Other than Simon, Skizzy, and Sara, there were few others Dagger trusted completely. Padre had to be kept at arm's length. Although they liked him, Padre was a cop first, and cops proved to be too inquisitive. "Well, I'm sorry you went through all the trouble to redecorate my office because I still don't trust you. You will just have to find someone else to do your bidding."

"We can be trusted. We kept your secrets."

"When it comes to you, I'm an open book. You molded me, trained me, even remembered I hated all those fake colors you used to create a more authentic atmosphere in your underground prison. That's why the black and gray décor." Dagger stopped. How did they know about his penchant for black and gray? "You've been to my house?" How could he be so stupid as to think he had heard or seen the last from BettaTec?

Another image popped onto the screen, the scene with Paul Demko in what looked like a hotel room, looking in a mirror, and straightening his tie. The image fast-forwarded and showed Casey at The Hideaway turning his head to the camera, a camera that had probably been on Demko's lapel or in his damn eye. Demko had stopped in to ask how to find a private investigator. More fast forwarding showed Demko jumping over the fence at Sara's property, then Demko fighting Dagger.

Dagger couldn't swallow, couldn't pull his attention from the screen. Tiny pinpricks tugged at the back of his neck. Could both Paul Demkos been equipped with cameras? He felt a familiar darkness start to rear its ugly head.

The next image was the Cardinal's hotel room where Sara had fought off Demko Number Two. The fast-forwarding slowed to real time where Sara ran at Demko. Glass shattered in slow motion, the image now of the outside of the hotel, Sara in a maid's uniform with a red wig, Sara falling toward the ground with Demko, then the wig falling away. In slow motion Dagger saw the shift from Sara to the gray hawk. The uniform dropped away as the hawk beat its massive wings and flew to the top of the hotel. Somehow the camera adjusted to a zoom as though someone were controlling it by remote even though it was in Demko's body. The hawk used its beak and pulled clothing from its talons. Another close-up showed those dazzling turquoise eyes. Then the image snapped off, probably when the vehicle and Demko exploded.

"We kept her secret," Connie said again in her robotic voice.

32 Minutes went by before Dagger found his voice. It was his job to protect Sara from outside forces who might discover her shapeshifting abilities. Her grandmother entrusted him with her safety. "What was your plan? Put the film on *YouTube* if I didn't help you? Do you think anyone would believe your film wasn't faked? They can do wonders with PhotoShop these days."

"True, but YouTube would not be an option. Sara, though, would be interesting to study."

Fuck me, Dagger thought. They could grab Sara anytime, anywhere, and there wasn't anything he could do about it. "The footage I'm sure has been seen by everyone at BettaTec already."

"Our sector filters and studies images before passing them on. We edited the film after the clone went through the hotel window. Easy to assume the camera had been damaged. We knew if the footage made its way into the wrong hands, they would consider Sara to be an interesting science project. We will try to keep them from finding out, but they have their ways."

"If I can trust you as you say, then you will destroy the video you just showed me." Dagger felt something evil coursing through his body. He walked over to the door and picked up the bat leaning against the jamb.

"We will."

Dagger hefted the bat, felt the sheer weight of it as something moved behind his eyes, the irises changing to various shades of darkness that rolled and tumbled and merged with the pupils. The rage had been fermenting for years. Whatever BettaTec had done to him, perhaps it had something to do with the chip in his neck, an uncontrollable rage took over his body.

"Do it now," he said in a voice that didn't sound like his.

"*After you do this one task. We would say to take your time and think about it. Unfortunately, we don't have that luxury.*"

"Here's my answer." Without hesitation Dagger swung at the monitor spraying fragments across the room. Then he clubbed the keyboard tray until it snapped off. He walked around the desk and took a swing at one of the legs. Wood splinters flew against the wall. He swung at two more of the legs until the desk tilted and crashed to the floor. The rugged desk shattered as though it were made of twigs. When Dagger had almost died from his encounter in Nebraska, Sara had found a vet who had used several pints of her blood to transfuse him. Her blood had given Dagger one of Sara's abilities—his wounds healed rapidly. Sara said he couldn't regenerate an arm or leg the way she could. However, by the looks of the way he demolished the desk, he wondered if he also had an enhanced strength the way she did, as though his beast needed any additional strength.

Dagger tossed the bat on the floor. "Fuckin' bastards."

Skizzy and Sara pounded through the door, then stopped when they saw the carnage. Skizzy said, "Got the locks. Did we miss anything?"

33

"How did you find this footpath?" Padre stepped lightly through the mangled grass. The sun slowly dipped below the horizon leaving behind a sky of red and purple hues.

"Satellite images. There used to be two roads into the worksite," Dagger explained. "Once the quarry closed, the roads and paths were only used by the occasional horny high school kids. The buildings are too far off that main road for anyone to notice."

Dagger had found it difficult to relax after his conversation with BettaTec. He had paced the acres back home like a caged animal, unable to get his mind to shut off, unable to reveal to Sara what Connie had said, how BettaTec knew about her, how he had let her down. To her credit, Sara didn't pressure him. Instead, she found him something else to focus on—Preacher. Once she piqued Padre's interest in the warehouse by the quarry, they had cobbled together a plan to make an evening reconnaissance.

Sara slipped into a pair of gloves. With the sun going down the temps were dropping fast. The cool air and the warm ground created a low lying mist.

"You do remember I totally dislike this quarry, don't you? Brings back bad memories of Luther and I using tweezers to pick up the remains of some guy who mysteriously blew up. Not one of my easier cases." Padre shuddered when remembering the Demko case. "I'd just as soon take a quick look-see at this warehouse and get the hell out of here."

"Come on, Padre. Where's your adventurous side? Don't I bring some thrill to your boring life?" Dagger slapped the cop on the back.

"I had a full head of hair when I met you, and because of you I went out and bought a silver crucifix to replace my gold one. Had it blessed by Father Frank."

"Silver to ward off vampires?" Sara said, finding it hard to keep the smile from forming.

Padre scanned the surrounding forest and the darkening skies, then made another sign of the cross. As they neared the large warehouse, they drifted from the path to the high weeds. They heard a loud hiss and a horn blast and saw a transport truck backing down the road from the main street. Two figures emerged from the warehouse and directed the driver.

"Come on," Dagger whispered. He made his way through the weeds to one of the windows at the back of the warehouse. They kept low and followed single file. The building was a cinderblock and metal structure left to decay after the quarry had closed down. There were actually three quarries connected making it close to two miles long and four hundred feet deep. History claims a meteorite carved out the quarries and that the quarries used to be a coral reef millions of years ago.

Dirt and grime crusted the window. Dagger poked his head up and peered through a corner of the window. The truck had backed into the warehouse and two men rushed to unload a shipment of cars.

"What the hell are they doing with those cars? They ain't even new." Padre squinted through the grime. Although there were only two lights in the warehouse, it was enough to make out various car parts scattered around the concrete floor.

Sara used her enhanced vision to study several of the car doors resting against a crate. "Look by the crate. Doesn't it look like they are stuffing bags of drugs inside the door panels?"

Padre used his sleeve to wipe a spot on the window. "How the hell do you see that far?"

"It's called youthful eyes, Padre, but she's right. That's what they are doing. Stealing cars, stuffing them with the drugs, and sending them across country."

"Not possible. Drug sniffing dogs would detect them."

"On one television show I saw them wrap the drugs in freezer bags then surround them with aluminum foil," Sara said. "Wouldn't that work?"

"Nah," Padre said. "That's television, Sara. Drug sniffing dogs have the best noses in the business. Coffee grounds, cayenne pepper, fabric softener sheets, nothing gets past the dogs."

"Come on, let's get out of here." Dagger turned and stared at two of the biggest Mexicans he had ever seen. "Shit. Could my day get any worse?"

34

"Tomas, what do we have here?" One of the men said. He wore an eye patch with a skull and crossbones painted on it. The other sported a black doo-rag on his head while coarse dreadlocks hung down his back. Although the air was chilly, they each wore camouflage wife beater shirts over camouflage pants. They were holding what looked like AR-15s with magazines at least a foot long.

"Looks like someone took a wrong turn." Tomas sniffed the air as though Padre emitted a scent. "I smell pig."

"I have back up coming in ten minutes." When Padre reached for his badge, Eye Patch waved the AR-15 at him to not move.

Eye Patch and Tomas traded grins while Dagger wondered how they had been spotted. They had stuck to the back road, parked a distance away, and thought they had been silent as they approached. Then he saw Sara lift her head and scan the skies. Very little sound ever got past her enhanced hearing. And then he saw it. A speck moving slowly above them.

"Drone? You have a fucking drone out here?"

Tomas smiled, revealing a mouth of yellowed teeth. "Ain't she a beaut?" He nodded at Eye Patch whose hands suddenly sprouted long, black zip ties. Tomas order them to turn around. When they hesitated, he pointed the weapon at Sara. "Now or I blow her head off."

Dagger and Padre slowly turned and placed their hands

behind their backs. Once Eye Patch had secured the zip ties, he had Sara turn around. She glanced at Dagger. One nod and she would spring into action, except Tomas had a gun pressed against her skull. He gave a slight shake of his head, so she stood still while her wrists were secured.

Once they stripped Padre and Dagger of their guns, they marched them to the front of the warehouse where two more guards were identically dressed, complete with AK-15s. They had their own little wife beater army going on as their dark eyes followed their every movement. They must have thought their little operation was safe from prying eyes. One was the size of a linebacker, and he hefted his cannon on his shoulder as though it were a baton. He tossed his sausage-sized cigar to the ground. A fireplug version of the linebacker mirrored his motions.

Padre smiled all friendly like as he approached. "Just checking for green cards, *amigos*. Then we'll be on our way."

The linebacker remained stoic. With a nod of his fat head, Eye Patch jammed his gun against Padre's back, sending him sprawling.

"You didn't have to do that," Sara said.

As Padre struggled to get up, the linebacker barked, "Stay there." He turned to Dagger. "You, kneel next to him." As though linebacker just noticed Sara, he ran his eyes down her frame, then slowly ran them back up again. "Was she searched?"

Eye Patch laughed. "You think she can hide anything in those pants?" He pulled her jacket open. "Nothing there but a nice set of *tetas*."

Padre flashed a concerned look at Dagger. With cannons pointed at their heads, they had few options.

The door to the warehouse opened and dammit if Ricardo Montalban didn't walk out. Maybe twenty pounds heavier and twenty years younger than the real thing. He could have been above-average looking if it weren't for the scar in the middle of his forehead.

"If a midget trails after him, I'm going to lose it," Dagger said.

"Well, well. We have a jokester. Pretty brave, my friend. What are you doing here?"

"We found them crouching in the weeds behind the warehouse."

"Lorenzo Hector Veradonez, aka Preacher," Padre announced. He studied the man's attire—black suit, white silk shirt, and a black silk ascot tucked around the neck. "You're Preacher, I'm Padre. We can open our own church," Padre joked. "How's the congregation?" Something seized Preacher's face and contorted it into a version of Satan Padre had seen in his youth in Sunday school books. "Like I told your boys, I'm here to check your green cards. I'm sure all your paperwork is in order and you certainly don't want a cop to go missing. It might send a shit load of cars out here."

Preacher snapped his fingers. The second hit came from behind again, catching Padre across the side of his head. He fell against Dagger prompting Sara to pull away from her captor. Three guns came up quickly, one pointed at Dagger's head, the other two at her. Dagger and Padre struggled to a kneeling position. Blood oozed from the side of Padre's head.

"Such a spirited girl. You guys are going to have your hands full." Preacher turned to the linebacker and nodded.

Two large tires came out of nowhere and were dropped onto Padre and Dagger. Before their fate could register, two more tires were dropped onto each of them while a can of gasoline appeared in Eye Patch's hand. His eyes were gleaming, and Dagger had a feeling he had the same grin as a kid putting the neighborhood cats on fire.

Sara's eyes widened when she saw the gas can. "What do you plan to do with that?"

"You'll get life for killing a cop," Padre yelled, as though any of these guys cared.

"Only if they find remains, which they won't." Preacher waved a hand at Sara as though shooing her away. "Do what you want with her, then kill her." This elicited broad smiles from Tomas and the two linebackers. Eye Patch fondled the gas can.

As they hauled her to the warehouse, Sara glanced over her shoulder at Dagger.

"Hey, babe. Don't take too long," Dagger yelled.

"Give me two minutes, sweetheart." Sara was pushed into the warehouse and the wooden double door slammed shut behind her.

"What's with the Lucy and Desi act when we're about to be roasted like marshmellows?" Padre's efforts to stand were futile. The tires were too heavy.

"We're just playing a head game, let the guys think we don't have a worry in the world."

"Well, it ain't working on me cause I'm worried." Padre struggled against the tires while spewing, "*Hijos de puta. Te veo pasar el resto de su vida en la carcel.*"

Preacher pulled out a cigarillo and placed it in a gold cigarette holder. He lit the cigar and glared at Padre through the smoke. "I doubt you will see us in jail for the rest of our lives, but if you feel better spouting threats, please go ahead."

For all the times Dagger cautioned Sara about shapeshifting where there could be witnesses, now would be a good time for her to break that code. He tried communicating with her telepathically, something they could do only when she was in one of her shifted forms. No luck. The sun struggled to cling to the horizon. If someone didn't turn on floodlights soon, they wouldn't be able to see a thing. Of course, fire wasn't one of the lights that came to mind.

Eye Patch held one can up and shook it. Frowning, he walked over to a stack of pallets where more gas cans were lined up.

"Aren't you going to at least fill us in on your operation here? We're going to die anyway so what would it hurt?" Dagger said as he stalled for time. "We already saw how you are stashing the drugs inside of the door panels. So how do you keep well-trained dogs from detecting the drugs?"

Preacher inhaled deeply, then blew a trail of tiny smoke rings. He smiled at his cleverness. "Ah, so curious. Guess it wouldn't hurt since you only have a few more minutes to live. If you were here tomorrow you would see that the cars are smashed up, dented, all compliments of muscle and a sledge hammer. They see no need to have dogs check a transport truck filled with cars headed to a scrap yard where they crush them for scrap metal."

Dagger struggled to free his hands while he gauged the distance between him and the AR-15 Eye Patch had placed on the pallet.

"Ingenious." Padre almost laughed at the resourcefulness of criminals. "You can set up distribution points just about anywhere you want."

"Enough with the talk, my friend." Preacher barely finished his sentence when one side of the wooden door to the warehouse exploded from the inside and Tomas came sailing out, landing on his side and rolling an extra fifteen feet. Two seconds later, the linebacker's body made splinters out of the rest of the door and he landed close to Tomas. The fireplug came scurrying from the opening with his pants around his ankles yelling a string of Spanish words too fast for even Padre to interpret. Sara strolled out holding the large cannon. Preacher's mouth slowly fell open and his fancy gold holder dropped from his fingers.

"Hey, Dagger. How does one of these work?" Sara barely touched the trigger and a spray of bullets hit the stack of pallets splintering the wood and sending Eye Patch and the fireplug diving for cover. Preacher flinched. "Don't even think about moving," Sara said.

She managed to hold the gun on Preacher while lifting the tires from Dagger. He felt Sara slip a nail under the zip tie and had no doubt her nail had turned into the hawk's talon which sliced the zip tie from his wrists. He then freed Padre from the tires and used his pocketknife to cut the zip tie.

Padre took a step back and gawked at Sara. "How did… how could…?" he stammered.

"That's my girl," Dagger said with a smile.

Sara shrugged. "Men are such weak mortals." Sara knew Padre would never understand how she could partially shift her hands into the hawk's talons to escape the zip ties, nor how her strength and agility could fling even a big bruiser like the linebacker thirty feet with enough force to demolish the wooden door.

"What's wrong with him?" Eye Patch's concerned voice grabbed their attention. Preacher's mouth hung slack, his body immobile, and his eyes frozen in confused panic. He remained motionless for several seconds. Then his body started to vibrate as though jolted by some unseen cosmic current.

"What the hell?" Padre took a step back as saliva started to dribble down Preacher's chin.

Sara called on the eyesight of the hawk. In the darkness she could see a line of red, like a laser, aimed at Preacher.

One on each side of his head, just behind the temple. She followed one of the beams with her eyes to a tree on the edge of the forest. A second beam came from the opposite side, also from one of the trees. She pierced through the leaves, stripped away the shadows and saw a figure dressed all in black. An identical figure lay hidden on the opposite side. They resembled Ninja's.

"Help him!" Eye Patch screamed as his boss dropped like a sack of garbage.

"Don't touch him," Padre said. "Maybe he was hit by lightning." He searched the sky for flashes of light. "Anyone smell ozone?"

Sara focused on the weapon, taking in the detail, the color, the shape. It didn't have a magazine, nothing for loading bullets. So what powered it and what was its purpose? She wanted to get closer, needed to get closer. Before she could move deeper into the weeds to shift, a scream diverted her attention.

Eye Patch stood frozen, his one good eye fixated where his boss lie twitching. Then wisps of steam started pouring from Preacher's ears, nose, and even the pupils of his eyes.

Dagger tried to make sense of it all as Sara cautiously approached the fallen man. Padre didn't have to worry about chasing down their captors. They were too shocked to move.

"Santa Maria Madre de Dios," Padre whispered as he made a sign of the cross.

35

Dagger's hair hung damp from the shower. He poured himself a tumbler of scotch and expected Sara to be showered and curled up in bed in a fetal position after watching what had happened at the quarry. Instead, he found her sitting on the couch, a glass of wine on the coffee table, a blanket around her shoulders. She had a pad of paper in her lap and a pencil in her hand.

Dagger took a seat on the couch next to Sara. Her eyes were intense and she barely moved her attention from the paper as she reached for the wine, took a long sip, then set the glass down.

"This is what I saw." She tilted the pad toward him as she told him about the two men in the trees dressed like Ninjas, holding weapons resembling the drawing. "I saw a beam from these weapons to Preacher. I wanted to follow them, see where they went. When I turned back, they had disappeared." She shook her head and took another sip of wine. "I should have followed them."

Dagger pulled the pad of paper from her and studied the sketch. Sara had a great memory for detail. He finished his drink with one long throat-burning gulp, then walked over to his computer and tapped a few keys. Less than a minute later Skizzy's groggy face appeared on the monitor, his gray hair sticking up on all sides, the ponytail sitting askew on the back of his head.

"What the hell in tarnation time is it?" Skizzy squinted at the screen. "Dagger, it's after midnight. This better be good."

Sara set the blanket aside, walked over, drink in hand, and stood by the railing separating Dagger's work area from the living room. She could see that Skizzy had fallen asleep in his bunker seated at the table where several computer monitors were gathered.

"Depends on how much you know," Dagger replied. "Have you ever heard of a gun that could heat the inside of the body but not show burn marks on the outside?"

"Huh?" Skizzy sat up, his eyes suddenly in focus. "What do you mean heat up?" He settled a pair of glasses on his nose and started pounding away on one of the keyboards. "I vaguely remember…" He scratched the stubble on his face then shook his head. "No, those are huge. There were Humvees with ADS mounted on them."

"What's that?" Sara asked.

Skizzy lifted his head as though sniffing the air. "That girlie? You two in bed yet?"

"Focus, Skizzy," Dagger said.

"Active Denial System was developed by the military for crowd control. It heats the surface of the targets, like the skin. Definitely not internal. Hang on." He tapped more keys, coaxing his computer to dole out information. "Maybe they redesigned it. However, it's hard to hide because of the size and leaves second degree burns on the skin. So unless they got really creative, I can't see how it is possible to…" Skizzy shook his head. "Gotta be something else. The ADS was designed to be a non-lethal weapon."

"What's the distance?"

"The beam can hit a target over seven hundred yards."

Sara asked, "Is it hard for someone to make a scaled-down version of that model?"

"Oooh, good question, girlie. I do recall..." Skizzy's voice trailed off again as his fingers moved faster than his mind. "The Silent Guardian. The L.A. County jail uses smaller units installed in the ceilings. It's good up to about six hundred yards. Again, it only heats the surface. Supposed to feel like touching a hot wire."

"What about something the size of a rifle?" Sara knew the Ninjas were holding what looked like rifles.

"That would be one helluva powerful weapon. Nothing I've heard about. Let me see what the boys have been working on." By the boys Skizzy meant the Defense Department. He had developed an easy back door into the DOD computers and could spy on the latest experimental technology.

"Get some sleep. You can work on it first thing in the morning."

36

"I tell you, I saw it with my own eyes." Padre gulped strong black coffee. He was on his fourth cup and it was only nine o'clock in the morning. "I know I'm trying to survive on four-and-a-half hours of sleep. Trust me, I know what I saw, and I'd sound like an idiot if I detailed it in my report." He watched Luther fire up his Stryker saw. "You aren't going to find anything there. I watched it float right out of his skull." Padre moved his fingers as though he were describing leaves floating in the breeze. "*Nada*. Nothing."

Luther glared at Padre, flipped down the face shield, and fired up the Stryker saw. Padre turned away and focused on something on the wall, the cup of coffee cradled in his hands. It wouldn't be the first time he had been vague when completing a report. And it actually couldn't be considered falsifying an official document. Preacher could have had a stroke, maybe a cerebral hemorrhage. It wasn't necessary for Padre to mention vapor oozing from Preacher's orifices.

The Stryker saw halted, Luther set it down, then carefully removed the skull cap. He took a step back and shoved the shield up from his face. "Damn. You're right."

John Wozniak filled the doorway, an ice pack pressed to his jaw and the other hand holding a mug. He hadn't bothered putting on a gown. "You sure as hell better stuff something in that brain cavity because I don't want to see empty space. Don't want to hear it. Just got through paying five big ones for a damn root canal. I am not having a very good day." Wozniak's jaw looked puffy. He popped a pill into his mouth, then washed it down with gulps of coffee, some dribbling down his chin.

"That's three now," Luther said. "Three missing brains and, according to Padre, they evaporated. Floated from their orifices."

"What about your guests in lockup?" Wozniak asked his detective. "Are they talking?"

Padre checked his watch. "Want to join me?"

John shook his head. "I got the DEA, FBI and all the other acronyms coming in to scour this scrap metal operation."

"Guess I could go rattle their cage on my own." Padre looked at the naked body of Lorenzo Hector Veradonez lying on the cold metal table. "What do I tell them if they ask how their boss died?"

John looked at Luther who shrugged. "A lotta stroke going around."

"I trust you had a good night's sleep." Padre set two cups of coffee on the table. His guest blinked, just one eye, and Padre tried not to stare at the eye patch. The other three prisoners had lawyered up faster than Padre could ask if they wanted cream and sugar in their coffee.

Eye Patch glared at the cup as though it were laced with truth serum.

Attempting a little TLC with the other suspects had gotten Padre nowhere. He had threatened to charge them with drug trafficking and weapons charges. Still, they weren't budging. Padre didn't care. He already had them on attempted murder; and since one of them was a police officer, namely him, he had an air tight case.

"I hope you can help me understand what happened to your boss. One minute he was standing there, the next minute…" Padre trailed off, seeing one eye blink, and the brow scrunch in thought.

"You tell me. I'm no doctor."

"How about your friends? Do you know their real names?"

His guest just smiled and took another sip of coffee. Padre was running their prints now, and he had no doubt they would all be in the system. "No problem. If you aren't in our system, I'm sure you'll be in the FBI's." This brought a strange smile to Eye Patch's lips which concerned Padre.

There was a knock on the door to the interview room. It opened and John stuck his head in. "Can I have a minute?"

"Be right back," Padre told his guest. He stepped out into the hall to see two men in dark suits standing at the end of the hall. "What's going on?" he asked his chief.

"The acronyms want all four of our guests. Figure if they can get them to roll on the guy at the top, they can put them in witness protection."

"You are kidding me, right? They tried to burn me alive." Padre shuddered at the memory of tires and gasoline. "They tried to kill a cop."

"My hands are tied. You know how it is. It isn't the first time we lost a prisoner to the big boys."

"Great. Just great." Padre walked away, leaving his chief to deal with the men from the various acronyms.

Dagger's computer emitted a familiar beep. "Skizzy must be done with his research."

Einstein tap danced on the perch on top of the filing cabinet. Without taking his eyes off the screen, Dagger reached into the desk drawer, pulled out a Brazil nut, and held it over his shoulder toward the macaw. He felt the daintiest of nibbles from Einstein's beak.

"AWRKKK. BITTER SWEET. BITTER TREAT."

"You are welcome, buddy."

A flutter of wings and Einstein took off for the railing on the catwalk. His powerful beak cracked open the Brazil nut sending the shell in two pieces onto the area rug.

"Thanks a lot, Einstein. You know where the garbage is." Sara picked up the pieces and tossed them in the garbage can.

Einstein cackled, a laugh that sounded a lot like Padre's. He clawed his way along the railing like a tightrope walker until he faced the tall windows and the view of the backyard. His head bobbed and weaved as he studied the scenery.

"Find out anything interesting?" Dagger asked.

Skizzy's scruffy face appeared on the screen. "And a good morning to you, too." Skizzy's eyebrows danced in opposite directions. "How does an HPM sound? It's a high power microwave weapon. Uses a continuous pulse wave, can go through walls. Not quite perfected and authorities don't understand them."

The hairs on the back of Dagger's neck started to do a jig. "Microwave, like a microwave oven. Something that can heat something on the inside and not damage the outside?"

"Depends how long you leave in your pot pie. It will all eventually burn. As I said, no one has been able to perfect it to be of any use, especially in something as small as a rifle. Most need amplifiers and microwave generators. I haven't really read much about it since nineteen ninety-seven."

Dagger's pen started dancing between his fingers, tapping on the desk in a rhythm as his mind starting playing the *what if* game. Although Skizzy could hack into just about every research department, it was possible something this high tech had been kept out of cyber space.

From behind him came Sara's voice. "Ask him if something high tech along the same lines could evaporate a brain while leaving the skin and skull untouched."

"What did girlie say?" Skizzy pulled his feet off the counter and shoved his face close to the monitor. "Is this what's melting those brains?"

Dagger told Skizzy how witnesses to Embuerto's death claimed they saw vapor or smoke drifting from Embuerto's nose, mouth, ears, and eyes. Then he told him about Preacher and how they had witnessed the same thing, along with Padre. All three of the victims, upon examination, were missing their brains.

"Holy sheeeit. Did I say that already?" Skizzy sat back and scratched the stubble again. "And it was quick you said?"

"Instantaneous," Dagger replied.

"Never heard of such a thing. Could that be dangerous or what?"

Dagger placed Sara's sketch on the scanner. "I'm going to send you a drawing of what this weapon looks like."

"You saw it?" Skizzy punched keys expecting the drawing to materialize from his printer.

"With binoculars. Maybe you can tell how the thing is powered." Dagger pressed the OK button on the scanner. "Look it over and also see if you can find anyone in cyberspace chatting about this thing."

37

"Just the guy I don't want to see." Padre motioned to a chair. "Where's your partner?"

"Sara's trying to wind down from last night."

"Smart girl."

Dagger flung himself into a chair and washed his hands over his face. "Well?"

"Same as Diego and Embuerto. Now we have all the acronyms crawling all over the warehouse and Embuerto's bar. It appears they were both doing the fancy car rehabs, transporting the drugs to various scrap yards. The acronyms are skipping like school girls. A filing cabinet in the warehouse had the addresses of all the other scrap yards." Padre leaned back in his chair and stared at his friend. "See anything that could tell us what the hell happened last night?"

Dagger didn't want to reveal what Sara had seen. Padre would want to know how she could see the Ninjas from so far away. He gave the cop his best trustworthy shrug. "Maybe the acronyms can find a strange drug in the warehouse. I have my best guy on the job."

Padre laughed at that one. "Right. Skizzy is probably still looking for an alien spaceship floating over the quarry."

"Actually, he has another theory which sounds strange and far-fetched, but we deal in strange."

"How strange?"

"Let us work out the details first."

"Great. It's better than having to look for someone who specializes in the Egyptian art of preparing the deceased for the afterworld." Padre turned to check the clock on the wall. "Think it's too late to start drinking?"

Dagger should have eaten something before going out with Padre for a few drinks. His head pounded like a jackhammer and his hands still shook from swinging the baseball bat against BettaTec's desk. BettaTec. Sara was right. The excursion to the quarry had been a diversion, even if for a short time.

He looked over at his partner sitting on the couch, her legs folded under her. She hadn't said much all night. Every so often he caught her looking at him. Shells from a Brazil nut dropped from the catwalk as Einstein flew over the couch and into the aviary. The macaw landed on a perch just inside the aviary door. He turned one yellow-ringed eye at Sara who gave the shells a passing glance and returned her attention to a magazine. She tossed the magazine down, gave Dagger another strange look, then walked to the aviary. Einstein raised one foot and clawed at the air between them as he hacked and hissed. This was unusual. Einstein only reacted that way around Sheila. Slowly, Sara slid the soundproof door closed, then as she walked past Dagger's desk she slipped the sweater top over her head and let it drift to the ground. Next, she unhooked her bra, gave Dagger a seductive look over her shoulder, then made her way to his bedroom.

Dagger should have realized this was completely out of character for Sara. His head told him to ask her what the hell she was doing, but memories of her naked body in the coffin got the best of him. He followed the trail of clothes to the bedroom, adding his own clothes along the way. He entered the bedroom to find Sara naked, lying on his bed, moonlight dancing across the most sensitive parts of her body. She held out a hand to him and he found himself on top of her, inside of her, pounding in a relentless fury. He should have questioned why Sara hadn't uttered one sound, not a moan, not a whisper. If was as though everything were mechanical.

Sara woke him several times during the night and he found himself wondering how his pure, inexperienced partner had suddenly become a vixen. Had Sara and Nick Tyler been closer than he had been led to believe?

A hint of sunlight streamed in through the bedroom windows. Dagger didn't think he slept one minute. Every time he drifted off to sleep, she had awakened him for another exhausting round. He turned his head to find Sara lying on her stomach, her silken hair drifting across his pillow, her naked body more tempting in the sunlight. He rolled on top of her, kissed the back of her neck, then froze. There, on the lower right side of Sara's neck, was a scar, identical to the one the Demkos had, the same kind that he had.

"What the...?" The anger slowly churned as his thoughts returned to last night and how strangely Sara had acted. He grabbed a handful of hair and spun her around while his right hand reached under the pillow and wrapped around his Kimber. He should have been suspicious. His Sara would have picked up the nut shells from her precious area rug. Einstein wouldn't have hacked and hissed at her. And his Sara would never have seduced him. Had BettaTec switched women on him?

He shoved the gun under her chin. "What did you do to Sara?"

The woman slowly smiled. She didn't have Sara's

turquoise eyes. How had Dagger missed that? She looked up at the ceiling with empty eye sockets and laughed, it was a taunting victorious laugh. Dagger felt his hand grip the gun tighter, his finger squeezed the trigger. He fired three shots into her face and heard someone emit a primal scream, suddenly realizing it was coming from him.

The bedroom door banged open. Dagger stared down at the bed, his hand wrapped around a pillow, his gun pointing at air. It had all been a dream.

Sara stood in the doorway with a cup of coffee. "Looks like you don't need caffeine this morning."

"Shit." Dagger fell back against his pillow, hands against his forehead, then looked at the gun. Something was missing—the clip.

"You really think I'd leave you with a loaded gun?" She walked out of the bedroom.

38

Dagger stood in a scalding hot shower, his mind replaying last night. Had it really been a dream or a warning? Had whatever Connie revealed to him in Nebraska finally sunk in? Was the dream telling him that he should be suspicious of the one person he had allowed to get close? Were her abilities really some Native American mythical talent or a creation of BettaTec? Could it have been by chance she had walked into his office seeking his help? If BettaTec had let him escape as they claim, then was it that much of a stretch to assume Sara was one of their plants?

He quickly dressed and found Sara in the kitchen leaning against the counter, arms folded. He pulled the carafe from the coffeemaker, poured a cup with shaking hands, then sank into a chair at the table.

"What did Connie reveal to you that has you acting so strange for the past two days?" Sara pulled out a chair cattycorner from Dagger and sat down. Dagger stared at her, studied her eyes, wondering which of them had the camera. "Okay," Sara said after his silence, "then tell me about the dream."

Dagger sipped the steaming coffee trying to decide how much to tell. He decided on the abbreviated version. "I dreamed that you had a scar on the back of your neck, like Demko. I thought BettaTec had abducted you and replaced you with a clone, someone with a scar on the back of her neck."

Sara turned and lifted her hair. Dagger hesitated, then leaned forward and studied her neck, checked both sides, then above the hairline. Sara released her hair and turned to face him. "Now do you want to tell me why you demolished the apartment? What did Connie say that set you off? It obviously triggered this dream you had."

He took a sip of coffee and let his eyes roam the back acres, the mums holding onto their fall colors. He slid his gaze back to Sara, sat back and slowly told her everything Connie had said. When he got to the part where he watched on the monitor how Sara had shifted into the hawk after plunging from the hotel room window, Sara straightened, a look of fear in her eyes. Her eyes shifted briefly to the eyes of the wolf. Just as quickly they shifted back.

"They know," she whispered, more to herself. She looked up sharply. "Do they know that the wolf kills any witness or how I can do a partial shift?"

"No."

"And they don't know about my blood, about what it did to you."

"No."

She nodded slowly, as though listening to assurances from some spiritual guide. "So this is what bothers you. BettaTec is so high tech you figured they created me in their lab somewhere."

"Crossed my mind. And now the dream. You said I read something off of the monitor in Nebraska, and if the numbers were embedded in my psyche, why not information about other agents?"

"Like me." She didn't say anything for several minutes, her eyes telling the story, how she finally understood just how dangerous BettaTec could be.

"I was six years old when I first realized I was a

shapeshifter. If BettaTec can create a past for you where you think you were a Navy Seal, ex-militia, attended the police academy, and whatever other lie they wanted to embed, they could have created a past for me. Maybe I didn't witness my parents' death. Maybe I didn't live on the reservation." She shook her head at the absurdity of it all. "That doesn't explain grandmother. She certainly didn't act like a handler. No." Sara shook her head again. "I know what I am and it isn't a BettaTec experiment." She studied him for several seconds. "So what exactly is it that Connie wanted you to do?"

"I never found out, other than something about some engineer being murdered and the killer is here in Cedar Point. Once they told me the leverage they had, I lost it. Destroyed the computer. Well, you saw the mess in the apartment." The anger had fueled the beast. How long ago had he arrived in Cedar Point? He had been searching for a safe town to hide in, a place to finally call home. "I shouldn't have stayed. Should have kept moving." His fist pounded the granite table. "I can't keep you safe this way."

"I think that I've proven I can take care of myself."

"You don't know these people."

"I don't think you do either. At least not Connie's division."

Dagger's phone rang. He pushed the speaker button. "What have you got, Skizzy?"

"I don't got nothin', but Casey called."

"Shit. I forgot to clean up the mess in the apartment."

"He called to thank you for cleaning it up. Says the place looks great. When did you do that?"

Dagger and Sara exchanged confused looks. "I didn't."

39

They found Skizzy standing at the bottom of the stairs behind The Hideaway. Dagger had asked him to bring his bug detector, the dead bolt locks he had purchased, and cameras to install inside and outside of the building.

They stopped in front of Skizzy and gazed up the metal stairs to the door to the office. Skizzy ran a hand over his stubble. "So the big bad wolf came to visit again."

Dagger pulled his Kimber from its holster and held it down at his thigh. "Let's do this." He was done playing *Mister Nice Guy*. Just like before, he doubted there were any warm bodies in the apartment. He led the way up the stairs and pounded his way into the apartment.

The three stood in the doorway to the apartment and gawked. Thick wainscoting lined the walls. Large black and white prints of landscapes had been hung. A new dark cherry wood desk sat angled in the corner of the room with two plush barrel chairs situated in front and a high back plush chair behind the desk. A thick area rug in a geometric gray and black design rested under the desk and chairs. A bookcase filled one wall and contained a collection of fiction and non-fiction books. The damaged furniture, rug, and even the broken bat were gone. A small refrigerator hummed softly against another wall near a bistro style bar in a corner. How thoughtful of BettaTec. Dagger snapped his eyes to Skizzy. The squirrelly guy immediately brought out his bug detector and set to work.

Sara took several steps down the hall and announced, "The bedroom has been redecorated, too."

Dagger stepped behind the desk where another business card had been placed. No name, no words. Just a picture of a betta fish. He crumbled the card in his hand.

Sara stepped close to Dagger and whispered, "What's the quote? 'Keep your friends close and your enemies closer?.' Let's play nice and see what happens."

"Are you sure about this?"

"Can't go back now. We're in too deep and they know too much."

Dagger waited for Skizzy to return with the "all clear" sign. "Install the outside cameras first, then work on the locks." Dagger waited for Skizzy to leave, then he took a seat in front of the desk and placed his thumb over the fish. A typing tray slid out and an embedded keyboard lit up. Again, there weren't any seams or lines on the desk, and this time the monitor appeared to levitate above the desk. Connie obviously didn't want him sailing a bat through a screen again. He typed in the IP address, then pressed the SPK button to turn on the speaker. A robotic face appeared on the monitor. Its eyes blinked and reminded Dagger of the robot in the movie, *I Robot*.

"You've been dropping a lot of money at IKEA," Dagger said.

"We failed to anticipate your reaction. Something that won't happen in the future. My apologies if you took my warnings as a threat."

"I take it your redecorating means you won't take no for an answer." Dagger watched as Sara moved to his side of the desk, slowly walking behind him, her eyes examining the monitor, checking for a camera which would enable Connie to see them. When she moved to the front of the desk and sat down, she shook her head slightly. She hadn't detected any camera.

"Just one word of caution, six-one-seven."

"I'm done with the past. Call me Dagger, NOT a fucking number," he snapped.

"As you wish, Dagger. As I stated, we need to trust each other. You probably are thinking of installing cameras in your office, but I do want to caution you that they will all be scrambled."

Dagger's jaw clenched as he stared across the desk at his partner. "I suppose that also applies to any cameras outside of the building?"

"Affirmative."

Dagger washed his hands over his face. He signaled to Sara and she immediately left to tell Skizzy not to waste his time putting up cameras. He sank back against the chair and noticed it swiveled and rocked. They had spared no expense. Solid wood desk and wainscoting. Even the area rug felt like it had the thickest padding available. Sara slipped through the entrance. Dagger could see Skizzy on the other side pulling out his tools to install the new locks. When Sara returned to her seat, Dagger contemplated his next move.

"I don't have to be a rocket scientist to realize that you didn't go through all of this trouble and expense for this task to be a one time deal." Dagger tried to hold the fury at bay, but it was hard. He had to get back into tai chi.

"*Unfortunately, we live in dangerous times and we need the best on our side. We may need help from time to time and will leave you a calling card when we need to speak.*"

"Which means you have someone right here in Cedar Point keeping an eye on my every movement."

"*Communication was always easier when your chip was operational. How you disabled it is a puzzle.*"

Connie obviously hadn't been able to figure out the value of the necklace and pendant he wore.

"Speaking of the chip, did the Demko clones have the same type in their necks? I'd just like to know in case I explode one day. It would be nice not to do it near innocent people."

"*After you escaped, the Director wanted to make sure we didn't have any other agents going rogue. He upped the ante, had nanobots implanted in all new recruits and existing agents. It's state of the art, sends back information on heart rate, blood pressure, other vitals. The nanobots also contain an explosive which Central Control can release into the body when necessary, like if an agent goes rogue or his mission is compromised, as were the Demko clones.*"

"Makes the betta fish aggression hormone my chip contained seem pretty archaic."

"*Unfortunately, it is something that has altered your*

genetic makeup and is irreversible. I'm sure you have noticed it yourself, as in the sudden destruction of our equipment."

Dagger had to again rein in the rage coursing through his body. He should probably be glad he didn't have the nanobots roaming through his veins. The thought of the Director implanting something like that into Sara infuriated him. "Just cut to the chase. Your blackmail has my full attention. What is it you want?"

"Blackmail is such a harsh word, Dagger. We prefer to say we have an...understanding."

"Right. Tomato...toomahto. Just tell me what crisis you are in the middle of."

"We believe...no, we know that Mason Godfrey is behind the murder of Keith Barent Johnson, the Raken Industries engineer."

"I'm not familiar with Mason Godfrey."

A video of a rotund man in a Wall Street suit, gray hair and dark glasses appeared on the screen, emerging from a private jet.

"Billionaire investor from Russia. He trounced through Europe driving down the value of each country's currency and making a bundle. Several countries have arrest warrants out for him. He sells himself as an investor, but we know he has his hands in money laundering, drugs and weapons. Half of Congress is in his pocket. He runs his drug trafficking business out of Afghanistan which is helping to fund terrorist activities. Godfrey loves making money; and if he can ruin

the U.S. economy in the process, he won't lose sleep."

Sara could see the video from her side of the desk. She was tempted to wave a hand through the suspended screen to see what would happen. An image behind the private jet looked familiar.

Dagger peered closer. "He's in the States?"

"Yes. We believe he is setting up a meeting with the final bidder somewhere in your area."

"To sell drugs? I thought you said he didn't get his hands dirty." Dagger saw a black Mercedes pull up next to the plane. The trunk popped open and a man emerged from the driver's side door. His dark glasses scanned the area before opening the back door. "Why here in the farm fields of Indiana? Why not L.A. or Miami?" Dagger was starting to believe what Padre once said—wherever Dagger goes, trouble follows.

"The low profile of the area has made it conducive to moving his drugs and weapons. It's a major distribution point."

"I don't understand. What does this have to do with the engineer? What on earth did this Mason guy have him working on?"

"Our sources have come up with more information. Johnson's parents were Russian immigrants. His father's expertise was military weaponry. Although deceased, we believe the father had a great deal of influence on the son. Whatever Johnson developed, it has drawn a lot of attention. Our contacts claim Mason Godfrey is opening the bid at one billion dollars. We think he tested the weapon's capabilities on Mister Johnson."

The image on the screen switched to the desert, to the same video Dagger had seen previously. The video replayed as Connie continued her explanation.

"Mason Godfrey will arrive at the Gary airport tomorrow and is renting a house on the shore under an assistant's name."

An address flashed briefly on the screen. Dagger memorized the address. "Wait. Put that desert scene back up on the screen," Dagger said. He knew Sara had seen it, too, because she got up and walked around to his side of the desk, wanting to see it from his angle. "Let it play out." They watched until the engineer's body stopped convulsing. This had been where the video had been stopped the first time Connie had played it. "I know what kind of weapon he developed." The vapor coming from Keith Barent Johnson's body appeared similar to what they had witnessed when Preacher died.

Murmurs could be heard from Connie's side, chairs shuffling, then silence, as though not to give Dagger the impression Connie wasn't alone. He knew they would never admit it. They never used real names and their identities were always concealed. If a computer could clear its throat, then Connie had just cleared hers.

"Explain please."

"HPM. A high-powered…"

"Microwave. I'm aware of an HPM. However, one has never been developed small enough."

"I already saw one. It's about the size of the Land Warrior, the corner shot."

"You saw it?"

"From a distance with binoculars."

The silence stretched to the point that Dagger wondered if everyone had left the room.

"In other words, your formidable ally saw it with her hawk vision."

Sara held back a gasp. Even though she knew they saw her shift into a hawk, she didn't think they knew of her abilities in human form.

Dagger ignored the comment. If Connie was trying to get a rise out of him, it wouldn't work. "I'm sure you have access to every police department's reports. Check the death of Diego Manuel, Embuerto Gomez, and Lorenzo Hector Veradonez, also known as Preacher. We had a front row seat to Preacher's death. You won't find anything in the autopsy reports other than vague reference to possible drug overdose, stroke or seizure. What the M.E. and police kept out of the reports is that all three were missing their brains. They vaporized and it was fast."

Other than a whispered "dear God," the silence stretched even longer. Dagger believed more than ever that Connie wasn't the only one watching him, making all the decisions. The female voice emanating from the computer could be a male's, for all he knew. They can do wonders these days with digital voice distorters.

After the seconds stretched into minutes, Connie finally replied.

"He has to be meeting the buyer in Cedar Point. He wouldn't chance trying to travel out of the country with the weapon."

"Weapons. Plural," Dagger added.

"Knowing the greedy sonofabitch he'll double his money with each buyer thinking he owns the only weapon. Once you have one weapon, it won't be hard to duplicate it."

"So you want me to find Mason and obtain the weapons."

"We need to know who the final buyer is and we need proof the weapons are destroyed."

A slight smile came to Dagger's face and dammit if it didn't feel as though Connie could see it.

"Mason Godfrey is not to be killed," Connie cautioned. *"He has others working with him. If he loses this battle, he will regroup and then we can discover the others."*

"Can't promise you that." And Dagger couldn't, not if it meant his survival or Sara's safety.

"We will rely on Sara to keep your dark side in check."

"My dark side?"

"Everyone is a moon, and has a dark side which he never shows to anybody."

"Mark Twain," Sara said.

"At least someone has read the classics. The long term outcome is more important than short term retribution. All we need right now are the weapons and the identity of the buyer. Godfrey should be ready to close the bidding."

"Any idea how Mason picked the lucky winners of his experiments? All three had something to do with drugs."

"There is a lot of skimming and territorial disputes in the drug business. As I said before, Mason is in it for the money. If any of the deceased were part of his network and dared to skim any of his profits, their days were numbered."

"I assume any buyer would be foreign. How would he get the weapon out of the country?"

"Diplomatic pouch."

"Something doesn't make sense," Sara said. "Why kill three people so publicly? Besides witnesses, now the authorities know there is something out there powerful enough to vaporize a brain. He's practically advertising the weapon."

"The same thought crossed our minds. Besides money, Mason also loves power. Imagine the control he could have over other governments if he just kept the weapons rather than selling them. Yes, it is puzzling."

Dagger noticed a slight delay between the time he asked his question and Connie replied. Skizzy would probably say the signal was bouncing from the apartment to a satellite and hundreds of relay stations while Connie watched from across the street.

"I need an update daily."

"When I have something to report," Dagger stressed. "If I set up a surveillance of this rental property, I'm not going to take a break to report in."

Another pause. He imagined Connie taking a hand vote from her ragtag band of happy warriors.

"Okay, when you have something to report." After another brief pause, Connie added, *"Seven, nine, four, seven. Half now, half when we have proof the weapons are destroyed."*

The monitor disappeared, the keyboard turned off and the tray receded into the desk.

"What was all that about?" Sara straightened and stepped from behind the desk.

Dagger looked over her shoulder at the framed picture on the wall of a forest of leafless trees, snow-covered ground, and a full moon on the horizon. He walked over to the wall and pulled on one corner of the frame. It hinged open to reveal a wall safe.

"That's creepy. What were the numbers Connie gave you?"

"The magic numbers." Dagger punched the numbers on the keypad. A red light flashed, then turned green. He turned the latch to reveal a one square foot safe containing stacks of banded money. They stared for several seconds and Dagger couldn't help thinking, "Once you take the money, there was no backing down. You're in for the long haul."

"Blood money," Sara whispered.

Dagger shrugged. "Payback. Maybe we can help Casey redecorate." He reached in and pulled out the bundles. "Gotta be about a hundred grand." After placing the money back in the safe, he slammed the door shut and swung the picture back into place. "I still don't think I have a dark side."

Sara gave him a withering glare.

40

Sara distributed cups of coffee while reporting on what she had discovered when scouring the Internet regarding Mason Godfrey. "One site labels him an eccentric billionaire who made his money in various business ventures. Helps old ladies cross the street, donates to all kinds of charities, has been married to the same woman for thirty years, had two sons. One died in a boating accident at the age of fifteen, the other helps him in his business ventures. He has lived in a number of countries. Became a U.S. citizen fifteen years ago. Nothing about the countries that want to put him on trial nor about any shady dealings. This, naturally, is from his company website, Godfrey Holdings Limited."

"What did the not so rosy sites say?" Simon asked.

"He has an art collection worth millions and denies rumors that they were stolen from Jews during the holocaust. His real name is Godfriejenski or something with lots of consonants. He's an arms dealer, drug trafficker, has bought and paid for a number of elections in various countries, all of which he denies and brushes aside as unsubstantiated rumors."

Skizzy rummaged through the bag of goodies Sara had brought from her pantry of home canned goods. At the bottom of the bag were containers of frozen meals. Chili, spaghetti sauce, meat loaf, and various soups. Sara always worried that Skizzy's diet consisted of coffee and canned tuna.

"At least Sara brought fresh coffee and donuts." Simon inhaled with relish his cup of Dunkin Donuts coffee. "Beats that battery acid Skizzy tries to feed us."

"You can always go to a restaurant," Skizzy yelled from the back room.

"What did you tell our neighborhood sheriff?" Simon picked through the box of donuts and grabbed a cruller. If Eunie could see him now.

Dagger cleared off the counter, making room for Skizzy's latest creations. "I clued him in on Mason Godfrey and gave him a theory about what killed the three victims. Naturally, I didn't tell him Skizzy was making replicas of the weapons or that I planned to steal the real things. I told him it was best he had plausible deniability. If I told him too much and he told his chief, Wozniak would share the information with the FBI, Homeland Security, and every other acronym. We need the deal to go down without any interference."

Skizzy emerged from the back room and set two rifles on the counter.

"What in hell tarnation are those?" Simon had held his share of weapons as a sniper in Nam, but he had never seen anything this elaborate.

Dagger picked up one and showed it to Sara. "How do they look?"

Sara studied the detail, recalling what she had seen the Ninjas holding. Skizzy had rigged a VHS-size black case on the side to resemble a power pack with a scope and laser sighting on the top. "You did an excellent job following the drawing. They should pass for the real thing, provided no one tries to see if it actually works. What about cases, Skizzy?"

"Standard black leather cases. If it doesn't match what he's using, then swap them out."

Simon asked, "What do you want us to do?"

"We're going to follow his limo from the airport, see where he's staying. When we know when the buy is going down, I'm going to need you two close by in case things go south fast."

"What about eyes and ears?" Simon asked.

Skizzy set a box on the counter containing several drones. "Once we know where the meet is, you and me," he waved a finger from himself to Simon, "will be within high-powered binocular distance away and send one of these babies to find a hidey hole on the car. I also have two mosquitos, one as backup in case the first one fails." He set matching ear buds next to the box. "We will be in constant contact so no going off the reservation, Dagger."

Dagger fought back a smile. "Sometimes you have to call an audible."

Sara set the rifle down on the counter and slowly turned toward the shuttered windows. She may as well have eyes in back of her head the way her radar worked. While the men continued fawning over Skizzy's invention, Sara made her way to the door and slowly splayed the blinds.

"What's the official cause of death on the three walking dead?" Simon asked.

"Massive coronary, drug overdose, seizure, take your pick. All hinted at. Bodies have been cremated. Cases closed." Dagger waited for Skizzy to open one of the black cases, then carefully fit the weapon into the foam interior. Simon did the same with the rifle he held.

"Still can't believe someone would invent this dangerous of a weapon," Simon added with a shake of his head. "You gotta get your hands on these, Dagger."

"That's what we plan to do."

"And you're sure Padre is able to keep the public and media from being suspicious? Is that ex-girlfriend of yours still sniffing around for a story?" Simon shook his empty coffee cup with a frown, then tossed the empty into a garbage bag.

"She's busy strutting her stuff in front of the DEA looking for an exclusive. That should keep her busy for a while."

"Not quite," Sara said from her position by the door. "She's outside leaning against the Navigator, obviously waiting for you."

"Blondie musta followed you." Skizzy grabbed the two black cases and carted them off to the back room. "Better get rid of her."

Dagger checked his watch. "Shit." He turned to Simon. "Can you give Sara a ride home? I'm going to find out what Miss Monroe wants."

Sara knew the hidden message in Dagger's comment. Sara had to get home so she could shift and the hawk could make it to the Gary Airport in time for Mason Godfrey's arrival.

Dagger slipped his sunglasses on and surveyed the surrounding area. Skizzy would have to drop off the fake vaporizers later. Dagger couldn't chance being seen in daylight carrying two rifle cases from Skizzy's shop.

"Well, well. If it isn't everyone's favorite mailman." Sheila had a flirtatious smile for Simon which quickly faded when she saw Sara. Just as quickly, her smile returned as Dagger approached. "You need to keep your vehicle clean, sweetie." She brushed imaginary dirt from the back of her red leather skirt. She fanned open the leather jacket and placed her hands on her hips leaving little to the imagination.

"Miss Monroe." Simon couldn't pull his gaze from her chest. "Those are some fine pencil erasers you got there. Who are you trying to impress?"

"Why you, my dear." Sheila tapped one finger under his chin.

"Simon, don't you have some place to be?" Dagger gave a nod toward Sara then turned his attention back to Sheila. "What brings you to the seedy side of town?"

Sheila stepped close enough to inhale his aftershave. She ran her hands down the lapels of his leather coat. "Just happened to see you drive by the bank and tried to call you. Changed your number again, didn't you?"

"Changed phones. I have a fondness for the disposable ones lately."

"Hmmm. And I don't suppose it would kill you to give it to me."

"That's why they call it disposable. Number changes too fast to bother sending out a Hallmark card."

"Bet Sara has it."

Dagger sighed. Sara's name seemed to be imprinted on Sheila's tongue. "Of course. She's my business partner. Let's not go into this again, okay? It's really getting old."

"The DEA is pretty tight-lipped about their witnesses. They plan to put them in the witness protection program while they work the case. They think there are links to some cartel in Mexico. I need a front page story, Dagger. You always have your ear to the ground. Hear of anything interesting?"

Dagger weighed his options as to how much to tell Sheila. At least it would keep her busy and out of his hair until he finished this latest project. "Why don't you do a thorough, and I mean thorough, background check on one Mason Godfrey."

"The billionaire?"

Why did that not surprise him? Sheila and her family probably knew everyone on the Forbes list of richest men in the world. Godfrey's wealth placed him far above the tight circle of the Monroes and Tylers.

"Just check out his background. The rumble is he's coming to town. You might even be able to scoop the DEA. Word is, he's up to his fat neck in the drug business, and I don't mean pain killers."

Dagger climbed into the Navigator and drove off.

41

The gray hawk used the wind currents to glide over the interstate as it tailed the limo from the Gary Airport. Three men accompanied Mason Godfrey. The trunk of the limo contained two rifle cases, one medium size suitcase and two small suitcases. Traveling light. The two body guards were similar in size to the two Ninjas Sara had seen.

Traffic was light this time in the afternoon. The toll road was the only major route through northwest Indiana. Weekends usually had the heavier traffic with people returning from their weekend cottages in Michigan.

Powerful wing beats lifted the hawk higher as it tried to assess the direction the limo was headed once it left the toll road. The lake looked pristine from this height. Trees were vibrant reds and golds and the temperatures were still comfortable. Most summer cottages, though, were either closed for the season or used infrequently.

"Earth to Sara."

"Bet you drove through McDonalds for a cup of coffee," Sara said in thought only.

"Yep." Dagger was parked in the driveway watching the map on the console. The blinking red light told him the hawk's location. *"Looks like you're getting close to the lake."*

"These are pretty big estates, each with about five to ten acres and each surrounded by fencing. Wait. The limo is turning down an asphalt road." The hawk kept a safe

distance away. Each estate appeared to have its own private road and enough trees on the properties to shelter the estates from prying eyes. The hawk circled offshore so it could view the beach area. *"Nice. Each of these mansions has a boathouse."* The limo stopped at a wrought iron gate. The driver checked a piece of paper and punched in a number. The gate opened. *"We won't be able to get in through the main entrance. There's a lake on the opposite side and woods on the other two sides. The lake may be the only way in."* Sara told him about the gate and keypad.

"I'll have Skizzy check out the address. See who the owners are and look for a blueprint of the place. See if there's an easy way in."

The hawk watched the heavy gate swing closed. A soft breeze swept leaves from the circle driveway as though in preparation for its visitors. Evergreens in various sizes looked recently trimmed. While the manicured lawn and well-tended shrubs of the mansion's front grounds were impressive, the area behind the house facing the lake served as the property's main focal point. There, the stairs of a large wrap-around porch descended to a patio leading to a fire pit, a perennial garden, and a boathouse which nestled close to shore.

"Interesting." Sara saw something else in the distance, an area void of trees with a brick path leading to the house. *"There's a helipad with a black helicopter. It's parked, no markings."* The hawk moved several feet down to a limb that hung close to the roof of the house. The limo driver quickly opened the back door to the limo. A man she recognized as Mason Godfrey stepped out. Thick eyebrows hovered over eyes that swept his surroundings at a practiced pace. Although the suit looked expensive, it appeared one size too small as he struggled to keep the jacket buttoned over

his portly frame. A slight bend to the nose looked as though Godfrey had enjoyed a few skirmishes in his youth. Grey hair was bushy and due for a trim. Even with his slovenly appearance Mason Godfrey had a regal air about him in the way he carried himself. The way he moved suggested everything in his path should step aside. Two men climbed out of the limo and joined them. The two were dressed in all black and were of medium height and build. The driver popped the trunk and the two Ninja's each pulled out a small suitcase and a rifle case.

"Is there any nearby structure where I can watch the house without drawing suspicion?"

"Given the seclusion of the nearest house and the wrought iron fences, it would be impossible to get close. You'd have to be on a boat in Lake Michigan which would attract too much attention."

"We can go in at night. I'll have Skizzy get us the blueprint and a raft. We can get in through the boathouse if the blueprint shows access into the house. Head on home."

But Sara didn't. Instead she kept a close eye on the black cases as the bodyguards trailed after Mason like obedient servants, lugging the contents of the limo's trunk while he carried his air of superiority.

The hawk moved to the back of the house and settled on the roof overhanging the patio. As expected, Mason stepped outside to survey the surroundings. He breathed deeply. The air must have been to his liking because he smiled and nodded his approval.

"James, how are we doing with the connection?"

The assistant stripped off his jacket and hat and now lugged a case and set it on the patio table. He pulled out a laptop, opened the lid, found an outlet and plugged it in. A vertical keyboard in the case looked more like an outdated phone. Mason pulled out a slip of paper and punched in several numbers.

"Is it all set to run?"

"Yes, Sir." James pulled out a chair and the portly billionaire sat down. James backed away and stood just outside the door should his boss need anything.

Mason studied the screen which showed a series of numbers. A wicked smile crossed his lips as he whispered, "Yes." The hawk moved several feet away so it had a clear view of the screen as the billionaire typed a message.

"You have the winning bid of ten billion. Bring one million dollars as a show of good faith. The rest should be wired to my Cayman Island account after you inspect the merchandise. Call when you arrive tomorrow and I will give you the address. Plan to meet at eight o'clock tomorrow night."

He pressed the send button then turned off the computer. "It's a go, James. Tomorrow night at eight."

The hawk moved to the top of a bird feeder a safe distance from the patio. It's acute eyesight could see the men moving around in the house. The black cases were in the foyer. One of the Ninjas picked up both cases and placed them in a closet just off the foyer.

The hawk lifted from the lamppost and headed over the water. The men paid little attention to the hawk as it sailed and dipped. After assessing the boathouse and its proximity to the house, it climbed and headed back to Cedar Point.

42

Simon was at the gate at nine in the morning. Dagger had already showered and filled Einstein's food dishes with fresh vegetables. He had been going over the plan in his head all night, tossing and turning, making notes on a pad next to his bed, even getting up and searching satellite maps on the computer.

He joined Simon and Sara at the kitchen table. The day was overcast, and according to weather reports, it would be overcast tonight, too, which worked out perfectly. They didn't need bright moonlight to announce their arrival.

Sara watched the two men load up their plates with scrambled eggs, potatoes, and bacon. "How can you two eat before a dangerous mission?"

Simon smiled around a mouthful of bacon. "Might be my last meal. Gotta make the most of it."

Dagger didn't say a word. The light in his eyes said it all. Sara gave up and filled her plate. "You two and Skizzy act like you are going on a fishing trip."

"It is, in a way," Dagger had to admit. He gave a nod toward Simon. "Is Skizzy ready?"

"Yep. He'll have everything in the Hummer. Will pick me up, then you two, around six. Should be dark by then. Take about a half hour to get there, maybe less the way Skizzy drives."

"You better keep him below the limit. We don't need

cops getting curious what he has in the back. What about the drones?"

Simon grabbed the carafe and filled his coffee cup. "Those are his toys. Has different kinds. Figure he'd send one to whatever car the buyer arrives in and the other he is saving for maybe the buyer himself. This way he can track where he goes." Simon waved his fork in the air. "What about an alarm system? Anything on the boathouse? Any motion detector?"

"No," Sara replied. "Nothing that I could see."

Simon's eyebrows tracked north. "Thought you couldn't get close?"

"Binoculars, Simon."

"Of course."

Dagger tried hard not to breathe a sigh of relief. "I trust the rubber raft Skizzy is providing doesn't have a leak."

"Already tested it. It's heavy duty. Deep enough well to conceal you as long as you don't pop your head up too many times. Got night vision goggles?"

"Really, Simon?" Sara said. "You have to ask?" Truth was, Dagger's night vision goggles were Sara's hawk eyes. He would still bring his own goggles, even though everything would be illuminated in a sickly green.

"Where will you set sail? Private homes means private beaches."

"There's a public access with a boat launch a mile down the beach." Sara gathered up the empty plates and carried them to the sink. "Hopefully, there aren't any night fisherman. With a raft, though, you don't need a ramp. You can drop in anywhere."

Dagger retrieved a satellite map that he had printed, which gave a good overview of the area. Simon cleared the carafe and cups out of the way as Dagger placed the map on the table. "This is the private road to the estates." He pointed to a wooded area a half mile away. "I don't see any fences around these woods and there is an unpaved road. That should get you close enough. No headlights going through the woods."

"We've got our own night vision toys." Simon pointed at the map. "That an extra copy?"

"Yes. My present to you." Dagger handed Simon the map and walked him to the door.

43

As promised the sky had remained overcast, not even a sliver of a moon peeked out from behind the dark clouds. Waves softly lapped onto the lakeshore one mile from the target. The crisp bite to the night air kept the boaters away. Dagger tapped his ear bud. "We're in position." Sara helped him drag the raft to the water's edge. They were dressed in black from head to toe including ski masks.

"Roger that," came Skizzy's reply. "Gotta perfect view of the drive leading to the house, although it's more like a goddamn fortress."

"Skizzy."

"Yeah yeah."

Simon broke in. "What do you want us to do while you're breaking and entering, wreaking havoc and having all the fun?"

Dagger suppressed a smile. Once a sharpshooter, always a sharpshooter. He understood Simon's itch to get into the game. "Keep an eye out for the guest of honor and be ready for a quick extraction. Make sure Skizzy has ears on the place and that he gets those drones to their targets."

"Stay dry."

"As long as Skizzy's inflatable raft doesn't spring a leak, we should be fine."

Dagger carried one of the rifle cases and Sara the other. They loaded them into the raft and shoved off. Skizzy had equipped the raft with an electric trolling motor and made it so silent that the lapping waves made more noise. Dagger adjusted his night vision goggles and a glowing green landscape appeared in front of him. As though Nature were aiding them in their mission, a mist drifted from the surface cloaking their appearance. Although all of the mansions they passed had boathouses, the adjoining piers had been removed for the season.

A raccoon crouched near a tree trunk on shore and stared at them.

"Don't even think of it," Sara whispered as Dagger reached for his gun. Two baby raccoons appeared from behind the mother curious about the strange visitors. A light clicked on in one of the houses revealing a wall of windows and a room full of plush furniture and museum size paintings. "The light is on a timer," Sara said. "There isn't anyone home."

"How's it going?" Simon said in Dagger's ear. "We don't hear you talking."

"That's because sound carries," Dagger grumbled. "Go dark."

"You can go dark, we'll just chatter away. So far no headlights headed your way," Simon reported.

"We see you, though," Skizzy chimed in. "Girlie don't have no night vision goggles. You musta only brought one set."

"Right." Dagger was breaking his own rule of staying silent. His ski mask and turtleneck were beginning to itch. As though that weren't enough, the odor of fish, seaweed and stagnant water from drained swimming pools assaulted his senses.

The raft rounded a corner and Dagger cut the motor. He grabbed the paddle and jammed it into the water, touching solid earth and stopping the raft. Lights illuminated the patio where one man stood smoking a cigarette. His jacket flapped open revealing a gun and holster. Tall trees along the property line leaked a wall of darkness across the water. Dagger kept the raft in the darkness as he watched the man pacing the property. He could see the helipad and helicopter a short distance away, just as Sara had described. Small round tables and wrought iron chairs dotted the patio. Other than the one guard, Dagger didn't see anyone else.

Sara tugged on Dagger's arm and pointed. "He was one of the Ninjas." The guard tossed his cigarette into the water and started for the house.

Dagger found the entrance to the boathouse and paddled in, careful not to make any noise. There were several ski boats and a speed boat stored in the boathouse. He figured anything larger must have been stored in a private facility.

Dagger maneuvered the raft to the stairs. Once Sara tied it to one of the cleats, she climbed out. Dagger handed her the two rifle cases, then climbed onto the concrete platform.

"Apollo has landed," Dagger whispered.

"Roger that," Skizzy said. "Still no oncoming traffic."

Dagger saw two doors. One led to the backyard and the second led toward the house one hundred yards away. Skizzy's blueprint hadn't revealed a boathouse so it must have been an add-on. Perhaps Sara was right. Perhaps the door led to an underground tunnel to the house.

Sara knelt in front of the padlock with a gun pick in her hand. Soon the rusted padlock snapped open. She slipped the padlock off, set it on the ground, then turned the door knob. The door opened with a scraping and squeaking.

"Idiots," Dagger whispered. "Don't they know not to use wood which swells and warps around water?"

"Good, it's a tunnel." Sara made her way down seven stairs to a damp walkway. As she had hoped, an underground entrance had been built so the rich little darlings wouldn't get wet when it rained.

Dried leaves littered the walkway as well as cigarette wrappers and burned out sparklers. "Looks like the hired help doesn't do tunnels."

"You two in position yet?" Simon said through the ear bud.

"Almost," Dagger said. They quickened their pace to a trot, the rifle cases slapping against their legs. They needed to find the real weapons and make the exchange before the buyer arrived.

The tunnel ended at another set of stairs. Sara pressed her forehead against the door and listened. She held up one finger. "I hear voices," Sara whispered, "not close by, though." She wrapped her fingers around the doorknob and turned. "It's locked." She used the gun pick again, then slowly turned the knob and opened the door a scant inch. Peering through the crack she saw a hallway that opened into a storage room of some type.

Standing behind her, Dagger whispered, "It's called a mud room. They change out of wet clothes here. There's probably a washer and dryer in the room, too. See any alarms?"

They both studied the doorframe for wires. Sara, using the hawk's vision, also checked for motion detectors. "Nothing," she whispered back.

Dagger pulled the door open and they slipped in, quietly pulling the door closed. Another door to the left led outside. He could see garbage and recycle bins in an area cordoned off in a cyclone fence cage, probably to keep the raccoons out.

Light spilled in from down the hall. Dagger pulled off his night vision goggles and stuffed them into an inside pocket of his jacket. The blueprints had shown a smaller kitchen on the opposite side of the house. He figured the industrial-sized one was for entertaining. It could mean Godfrey and his entourage wouldn't be accessing this side of the house.

They made their way down a tiled floor, the larger kitchen on their left. A small light above the sink cast hulking shadows across the room. Dagger was regretting taking off the goggles. Anyone could be waiting in the kitchen and he hadn't even thought of a guard dog. Sara's previous reconnoiter confirmed Godfrey's only travel companions were two-legged.

Sara suddenly grabbed Dagger's arm. "Someone's coming."

44

Sara saw a pantry to their right and pulled Dagger into the opening. They pressed their bodies against the wall as the footsteps grew closer. Dagger pulled the Kimber from its holster and quietly affixed a silencer. The footsteps stopped several feet away, then a light snapped on spraying light across the hallway. They looked in horror at their footprints on the tiled floor. They had stepped in wet sand when launching the raft into the water.

They heard the sound of a zipper, then water splattering into a toilet bowl. A loud sigh echoed in the dark as the man relieved himself. A toilet flushed, then the light turned off and footsteps receded. Dagger breathed a sigh of relief that the man hadn't noticed the footprints. Sara was appalled that the man hadn't washed his hands.

When the footsteps faded, they emerged from their hiding place and proceeded down the hall. Muffled voices could be heard, along with the crackling of a fireplace and scent of wood burning. Sara listened briefly, then held up three fingers to Dagger. The hallway curved at the front of the house. Blinds were closed on the wall of windows to their left. On the right dark paneling served as a divider with open slats every four feet. From the outside the house had appeared two-story. Once inside, though, they saw the vaulted ceilings.

They approached a large entryway. With his back pressed

against the paneled wall, Dagger took a quick peek through one of the slats. Mason Godfrey lounged on a couch in front of the fireplace like Jabba the Hutt. He held up a glass of wine as though appraising the contents. One of the Ninjas stood behind the couch, waiting for the next command. A third man sat on a chair next to the couch, a briefcase near his feet. They could only assume the other Ninja was outside waiting for their guest. There were three groupings in the large room and Godfrey was seated in the one farthest away. His voice reverberated off the high ceiling.

"Bring the weapons here, Saul."

The Ninja nodded and headed toward the entryway. Dagger and Sara just made it to the pantry when Saul entered the hallway. He opened a closet door and there were the two rifle cases.

A muffled voice from a walkie-talkie blurted, "We have a car headed this way."

"Got headlights," Skizzy said in Dagger's ear.

"Little late on the uptake, Skizzy."

"Bite me," came the reply.

Godfrey barked, "Saul, go meet our guests."

Saul set the cases against the wall and rushed down the hall to the front door. Dagger heard a door open. They waited several seconds, then heard more talking near the front of the house. They crept back to the paneled wall. Godfrey stood gazing out of the wall of windows toward the lake, hands clasped behind his back. The emperor waiting for his subjects.

"Hurry," Dagger whispered. They quickly exchanged the cases and crept back to the pantry.

Loud voices could be heard from the front of the house. "Welcome. It is so wonderful to finally meet you. Oleg, get our guests something to drink."

Footsteps could be heard. Saul appeared, swooped up the cases, pushed the closet door shut, and hurried into the great room.

"I think there are two visitors, no three," Sara whispered. "The guest called someone Fredrik and also mentioned a driver." Once they could no longer hear voices in the foyer, they moved back to the paneled wall.

"Releasing drone one," Skizzy announced. "It's headed toward the monster Caddy."

Mason Godfrey held up a cigar to his guest who shook his head. "Do you mind if I do?"

"Actually, yes, I do. Allergies." The guest was tall and distinguished looking with a full head of well-sculpted salt and pepper hair. He stood ramrod straight which made the word *military* come to mind. A wiry man, who looked more like a butler, stayed within arm's length. He introduced his assistant as Fredrik. Another man stood just inside the doorway, his eyes assessing Godfrey and his entourage.

"Of course." Godfrey stubbed the cigar out in an ashtray on the coffee table. He then introduced his assistant, James. Like a proud father he motioned to the two Ninjas. "Oleg and Saul had the pleasure of testing the weapons, as you saw in the videos I posted." He clamped a beefy hand on his guest's arm and pumped it for all it was worth, all ten billion dollars worth. "The illustrious Jonathan Keyes. It is a pleasure to finally meet you."

"Jonathan Keyes," Dagger whispered as he dug deep into his memory bank.

"What's wrong?" Sara whispered.

Dagger glared at the guest through the slatted wood panel. He pulled out his cell phone and started snapping pictures. "Where have I seen him before?"

"What?" Sara used the hawk's vision to zoom in on

the man. Dagger was right. He did look familiar. But from where? She focused on Fredrik who stood only a few feet away, his eyes staring at Godfrey. Something on his neck drew her attention. She covered her mouth to choke back the gasp, then leaned in close to Dagger. "Fredrik. He has a scar on the back of his neck."

The recollection hit them both. They had seen a halogram of Keyes in the underground city in Nebraska. Godfrey's guest, the man purchasing the weapons, was the Director of BettaTec!

45

Dagger pulled the Kimber from its holster, his eyes showing a rage Sara knew all too well. "No!" She clenched his arm so tight Dagger winced. "Let this play out. We have to find out what he planned to do with the weapons."

"If Connie knew…"

"Knew what?" Skizzy's voice piped up. "What's happening?"

"Later," Dagger said through clenched teeth. Sara forced the Kimber back into the holster.

"Did you bring the good faith money?" Godfrey asked as James opened a laptop, set it on the coffee table and punched several keys.

The driver appeared in their line of sight carrying a satchel. He unzipped the satchel, pulled the handles to show the cash. "One million, as requested," Keyes said.

"Saul, the weapons." Godfrey motioned to the two cases on the floor. Saul picked them up, but neither Fredrik nor Keyes' driver made a move to take them, so Saul placed the rifle cases on the couch.

"I'd like to see the schematics first." The air between them seemed to crackle as the two men faced off. Keyes knew Godfrey would never let the schematics out of his sight.

"As you wish." Godfrey opened a briefcase, unzipped the top liner, and pulled out a rolled paper. He handed it to Keyes who unrolled it and gave it a quick glance.

"He has no idea what he's looking at," Dagger whispered. How could anyone? The weapons were state of the art.

"I have the routing number for my off shore account." Keyes reached into his inside pocket. The driver moved away from the doorway and closer to the couch where the weapons lay. Perhaps Mason's over-confidence prevented him from noticing how Keyes' men had positioned themselves.

Events unfolded quickly. Before Oleg or Saul could react, the driver had a stun gun in each hand and felled the two men. Fredrik did the same to James while Keyes held a stun gun against Mason Godfrey longer than needed.

Four men down in less than seven seconds. Keyes raised an eyebrow as he assessed the situation. He handed the schematics to Fredrik who placed it in a tube, then into a briefcase. They walked out in single file, leaving the four men twitching on the floor.

"I don't understand," Sara said. "They left the weapons." She moved from the wall and tried to see where the men had gone. "Maybe they are coming back for them." Then they heard car doors slam and a vehicle tearing down the drive.

"Hell, they even left the one million dollars." Dagger shoved his phone back into his pocket.

"A million bucks?" Simon squeaked. "Who the hell leaves a million bucks behind?" After several seconds Simon added, "Unless it was counterfeit." After another pause Simon said, "Or maybe there's more than money in that bag."

Dagger and Sara exchanged looks. "Oh shit," Dagger said. They tore down the hallway, past the kitchen and through the mud room. Rather than taking the long tunnel to the boathouse, they went out the side door by the trash containers, across the lawn, their arms cradling the rifle cases. What if they were wrong? What if they had just left one million dollars sitting in the mansion? And why only use a stun gun on the men? Was killing them against some villain code of ethics?

A thunderous explosion forced a wall of hot air against their backs, lifting them into the air. The rifle cases flew out of their hands and the ground came up fast. Dagger saw the inky black water first. He reached out a hand, grabbed a fistful of Sara's black pullover, and wrapped his arms tightly around her as they both hit the water. They landed fifty yards from the scene in a shallow part of the lake. The chilly waters numbed their bodies instantly, but adrenaline helped them claw their way to shore. They rolled onto their backs to catch their breaths. Dagger felt as though every rib in his chest just realigned. Another explosion sent more fiery debris into the sky. Trees caught fire quickly as burning rubble rained down. The mansion looked as though a large behemoth had stomped on it with both feet. Bricks and the foundation had been reduced to rubble. The force of the blast had leveled every tree and fence surrounding the estate. Another fireball shot up sending debris from the helicopter into the sky. Dagger and Sara heard a whooshing sound, like a huge fan had just been switched on. Then they saw them, the helicopter blades cutting through the air, spinning wildly right toward the shore.

"HOLY SHIT!" Dagger knew they couldn't move in time so he tried his best to shield Sara. He heard a crunching sound and felt a spray of sand and water churning as the blades cart-wheeled along the shore.

They opened their eyes, then turned and looked behind them at the shaved trees, the ripped ground, and the helicopter blades stuck in a metal storage shed in a neighboring yard. They cautiously sat up, not sure if their bodies had been sliced in half. Somewhere along the way they had lost their ski caps. Dried leaves and twigs were finding safe haven in their hair.

The sky remained ablaze with fire and smoke. All around them, as far as they could see, stone, roofing, timber, and scraps of what once were the furnishings of the mansion, littered the ground. Soon the place would be crawling with rescue vehicles.

"Hey!"

Dagger turned to see Simon hauling ass down to the shore. They each picked up a rifle case. "Hey," Simon repeated. "You two okay?"

The Humvee barreled through the downed fence and trees and rumbled close to shore. Skizzy staggered out, surveying the surroundings, the trench the helicopter blades had made several feet from Dagger's head. "You sure as hell know how to make a mess. Stop lying around. Let's get going."

Simon tossed the cases in the back of the Humvee and retrieved a blanket which he tossed at the drenched and shaking duo.

Dagger and Sara huddled in the blanket, their bodies shaking from the adrenaline and wet clothes. Through chattering teeth Dagger summarized what had transpired at the mansion. "What about the drones?"

Skizzy punched a button on the console. A map lit up showing a pulsing blip. "Got a lady bug behind the license plate."

"And the other?"

"I figure after we drop you two off, we'd take a look-see where the limo is going. Maybe have it implant a tracker in the boss man's neck."

"No. Not him. His assistant."

"The stiff-as-a-statue looking dude?"

"Yeah. He already has a scar on the back of his neck so it will mask the chip you implant. I know how BettaTec operates. A chip in the Director's neck would set off too many alarm bells."

Simon turned from his seat. "A scar? You mean like those Demko twins?"

Skizzy's eyes looked bugged as he stared at Dagger through the rearview mirror. "Another clone?"

"No. Just another trained monkey."

"We checked the airport while we were waiting. The pilot hasn't filed another flight plan so we don't think this guy is leaving town just yet," Simon said.

"He has the blueprints, wasn't even interested in the weapons." Dagger paused while another wave of the shakes racked his body. Sara, on the other hand, hadn't said much since the explosion. "We need to work in shifts. I have a plan."

Simon chuckled and shook his head. "Of course you do."

46

They stumbled through the kitchen door and stood for several seconds listening to the blessed silence. Their hair and clothes reeked of smoke and damp wool. Dagger leaned against the wall breathing as though he had just finished running a marathon. Slowly, they kicked off their shoes, first one, then the other. Next came the wet socks. The tiled floor felt cold against their bare feet.

For the first time since the explosion Sara spoke. "Every time I close my eyes I see those blades cutting through the air right at us."

"I know."

She pressed her forehead against his chest, could hear his heart racing, feel the blood pulsing through his veins. "I thought we were both going to die."

Dagger tried to stop his body from shaking. After all, he was supposed to be the strong one. How many of his nine lives did he have left? How many times was he going to put Sara in danger? "You could have saved yourself, Sara. You could have shifted, moved out of the way."

Her head shook from side to side. "Not without you. I didn't want you to die alone."

Sara lifted her face and stared into eyes that were as dark as night. Dagger flicked pieces of twigs and grass from her hair. Even dirt smudges didn't take away from her beauty. He had fought for so long to push back against the growing affection. She would die for him, something she had proven on a number of occasions. Her blood coursed through his veins. Even now, her mouth so close to his, she was inhaling as he exhaled.

Dagger's mouth hovered over hers, and he felt the room starting to spin, their breathing in a measured rhythm. He knew adrenaline could push people to do something they might regret. Sharing a death-defying moment could do the same. His brain said to put the brakes on, but his heart argued it was inevitable. He wanted to ask if she was sure about this, but too afraid she'd say "no." He tasted her lips, giving her a chance to back away. Instead she moved closer, grabbed a fistful of his jacket. Then the urgency was too powerful. The kiss was deep and passionate, lips barely parting as they clawed sweaters and turtlenecks from their bodies. They circled in a slow pirouette into the living room, dropping pieces of damp clothing on the tile floor. Buttons flew across the room and zippers ripped as they rushed to remove the last of the clothing.

"My bedroom or yours," Sara breathed.

Dagger drew in a ragged breath as his eyes swept up the stairs to her bedroom…too far… and across the wide divide to his bedroom door. "Hell, I'm not going to last that long." He lowered Sara to the floor.

"Wait! My rug."

Dagger yanked the blanket from the couch and flung it on the floor. Damn her area rug, but he had to smile. At least now he knew he wasn't dreaming.

47

Dagger pried his eyes open from the sunlight streaming through his bedroom windows. His body felt battered and bruised. They had moved from the living room floor to a hot shower, then a long hot soak in the whirlpool, Sara with a glass of wine and Dagger with a tumbler of scotch, then to Dagger's bed. He studied the naked body next to him. Sara was lying on her side, her back to him, her hair spread across the pillow. He frowned as the image appeared similar to his dream. He rolled over and carefully pulled her hair away from her neck.

"Did I grow a scar overnight?" Sara said.

Dagger kissed her neck and smiled. "No."

Sara rolled toward him clutching the sheet to her naked body. She wove her leg around his and sighed. "What's on the agenda?"

"We're going to go have a heart-to-heart with Connie."

"Is your phone still intact?"

"Yes. It didn't get wet. I just have to figure out how to upload the pictures. We can catch breakfast in a drive-thru while Skizzy fills us in on what's happening at the hotel."

"So case closed, almost."

Dagger stared at the ceiling, his thoughts back to another time when he had pressed against Sara's naked body. "Except we still don't know who drugged us and put us in that coffin."

Sara looked up at him with those dazzling eyes. "I'm pretty sure I have it narrowed down to a prime suspect."

Dagger cocked his head, trying to prompt a response. "Well?"

"I think I'll let you torture it out of me."

It took him all of three minutes to get the answer.

"Where are you headed off to this morning?" Eunie, still clad in her terrycloth robe, poured Simon another cup of coffee. She pulled the bowl of scrambled eggs toward him as she took a seat.

"Just waiting for instructions from Dagger." He sighed as he admired the changing colors in the surrounding trees. The jalousie windows were open a crack, and the air was filled with the scent of burning logs.

The kitchen nook had a fabulous view of Lake Michigan in the distance. Eunie had always wanted a rustic log cabin with a view of the dunes and lakeshore. The house wasn't located in a gated community nor was it a seven figure estate that would raise eyebrows since a postal worker barely making sixty thousand a year could hardly afford a house the size of the Tylers' or Monroe's. Instead, Simon could show a sizeable inheritance from an uncle which permitted him to pay cash for the three hundred thousand dollar cabin, thanks in part to Skizzy's computer magic and Dagger's generous thanks to the two men who aided and abetted his ventures.

Eunie knew of Dagger's generosity. She also knew Dagger wouldn't do anything to get Simon in trouble. Even on the off-chance Simon did, she knew Dagger would do everything he could to get her husband out of a jam.

Simon's eyes twinkled as he studied the love of his life. "So, Eunie. You haven't said much about your college friends who came in for that conference."

"That weekend came and went so fast, I swear. I enjoyed

seeing them again." She lathered an English muffin with cream cheese, then took a dainty bite. She nudged the bowl of fruit in his direction.

"Hmmm." Simon waved a piece of bacon in the air. "That one woman, she's a doctor or something right?"

"Carol? An anesthesiologist."

"Pediatrics, right?"

"Yes." Eunie took a bite of the English muffin, a smile playing at the corners of her mouth.

"And the other lady, Joy was it?"

Eunie nodded. "She's a hospice worker." Her hands moved the platter of bacon closer to her husband. "You met them briefly when they stopped by. Why the interest?"

"No reason." Simon grabbed three more pieces of bacon. He preferred real bacon; but Eunie worried too much about his health, so she plied him with turkey bacon and Egg Beaters. He watched his wife's eyes dance around a kitchen filled with a crafter's touch. Pots were suspended over the island work station and rooster figurines were perched above the cabinets. He had left all of the decorating to Eunie and, boy, that lady loved to shop.

"They were some pretty hefty ladies."

"Now, Simon. That's a little brash coming from a man who tips the scales close to two hundred."

"Just saying, seems to me those two would have no problem lifting a one hundred eighty pound man."

Eunie didn't have to say anything. The twinkle in her eyes said it all.

"I believe," Simon continued, "that the one friend, Joy, her uncle owns a cemetery out in LaPorte, doesn't he?"

Eunie's smile widened, and still she said nothing.

Simon's chuckle started low, then grew as Eunie's smile grew. "I am curious how you pulled it off. How did you get them to the restaurant? And how did you convince Dagger to go anywhere without that gun of his?"

"Now Simon. Aren't you the one who always said you never want to know how they make hotdogs? Well, this is one of those times. It's best you not know the details."

"Oh no. You aren't going to leave me in the dark. Now tell me all the gory details." He loaded more scrambled eggs onto his plate as though needing nourishment to get him through her long explanation."

Eunie squirmed like a school girl as she set her English muffin down. "Dinner was easy. Sara mentioned it to me a week ago that they were going to dinner there. All Joy had to do was rent a limo. Gregory, her husband, had a college friend who ran a fleet of them. With a tux and a fancy British accent, Gregory could pass for a palace guard."

"But why didn't Dagger take his Navigator? Why did he borrow Skizzy's Cadillac?"

"You will have to ask him that, although Sara has said before that Dagger often helped himself to Skizzy's vehicles." She leaned closer, even though they were the only two in the house. Her eyes were lively, and it was all Simon could do to keep her from launching from her chair.

"This is where the plan almost fell apart. Gregory waited in front of the hotel right by the limo. Soon as he saw Sara and Dagger, he offered them a free ride to the Dunes to see the meteor shower, compliments of the hotel. Well, Dagger wanted no part of that. He had his car and could care less. Gregory started to panic. He knew not to push hard because I told him Dagger would get suspicious. Well, those meteor gods must have been shining down on us because Dagger's car, or whatever car he used, was stolen right from the parking lot. He came trotting back to the front of the hotel and took Gregory up on his offer."

"What about the hotel room? You only mentioned dinner."

"First things first." Eunie stretched out the suspense by taking time to refill her coffee and spread more cream cheese on her English muffin. "When Dagger insisted on going home, Sara batted those baby blues and before you know it, they were off to the Dunes. Naturally, Gregory had stocked the limo with scotch for Dagger and Frangelica for Sara. Water, too, all laced with Carol's special mix."

Simon's eyebrows raised with concern. "That could have been dangerous, Eunie. How could Carol know how the drug would react on them? And how come neither of them remembered anything they did prior to the limo ride?"

"I trust Carol. She said it was safe even though it blocked the memory. Eventually they will remember events prior to the limo ride, but that's it. Anyway, the team met at the cemetery. Once they had the couple safely cocooned in the coffin, Gregory called using Dagger's credit card and made the hotel reservation. He checked in and he and my friends left all the clothes and other possessions in the hotel room, along with the key card. Case closed."

"My Lord. I didn't know I married such a devious woman."

Eunie leaned over and kissed his cheek. "Not devious, honey. Just a hopeless romantic."

48

As he watched the scene of the explosion, Dagger called Skizzy for an update. "What's the latest?"

"Your guys are holed up at the Beach Front Suites, eighth floor. I have a room on the eighth floor of the Hilton Oasis two blocks away with a great view into the suite. This baby breaks down pretty easily. I was able to carry everything in a suitcase rather than a rifle case."

"Any movement?" Dagger saw a crowd of emergency vehicles along the road leading to the crime scene. Smoke still spiraled in several places, but it didn't prevent the emergency crew from removing two body bags.

"I got ears on them. He's expecting a visitor at one o'clock. A guy by the name of Isaac Boransky. Ever hear of him?"

"No."

"Well, stars align. This guy is some big shot in the Russian KGB. Says he's bringing a scientist with to authenticate the schematics. Your boss is selling the freakin' blueprints. Didn't see that one comin', did ya?"

Dagger washed his hands over his face. "Nothing the Director does surprises me. And don't refer to him as my boss, dammit." He looked over at his partner. Sara picked through her drive-thru breakfast like a prospector searching for the tiniest nugget. She didn't care too much for fast food, was suspicious of the yellow stuff that passed for scrambled eggs, and had shaken everything off, preferring to only nibble on the biscuit. He would have to buy her a sensible meal once this whole mess was through.

"Hey! You still there?" Skizzy's voice blared through the speaker. "As it is I thought you were supposed to call an hour ago."

"We got delayed." He knew without looking that Sara was smiling. Truth was, they had taken a long sudsy shower after he had tortured Eunie's name out of her. He had promised not to confront Eunie, especially seeing that a more sinister plot hadn't been behind their abduction.

"Well, Simon is going to be here in a few minutes to take the second watch. Want me to stick around?"

"No. Go home and get some sleep." Dagger pushed the off button just as someone rapped on the side window. Dagger turned his mirrored sunglasses to see Padre pointing at the back seat.

The cop climbed in and slammed the door shut. His rumpled trench coat looked worse for wear. "Nice and warm in here." Along with crisp air, fumes from the explosion clung to his clothes. "I'm sure you have a wonderful explanation. You want to tell me what you are doing here?"

Dagger shrugged. "Boring day. Thought we'd go for a ride. Saw the flashing lights and thought we'd see what was shaking."

"Uh huh." He patted his pockets and pulled out a pack of gum. He offered it to each of them, but they declined. What he wouldn't give for a cigarette.

"Looks a little warmer over there." Dagger pressed his back against the car door in order to see Padre better. "Someone leave their fireplace unattended or decide to torch the place?"

"Arson wouldn't have blown bricks over a quarter mile

away. Even demolished the helicopter."

"Maybe a gas leak. Were the owners home?"

"Fire Department called the owner's cell. He's in Boca Raton for the winter. Said he rented his place out to a James Franklin."

Dagger gave a nod toward Luther's M.E. wagon. "I see they found bodies."

"Two unlucky souls." Padre unwrapped the gum and proceeded to savor the taste, pretending he was inhaling his favorite cigarette.

"There should be four bodies in there," Dagger said. He turned his attention back to the chaos at the beach which could be easily seen now that the bomb uprooted almost every tree that had surrounded the mansion. He heard a heavy sigh from the back seat, pulled off his sunglasses and tossed them on the center console.

"Sonofabitch." Padre raised his eyes skyward. "Sorry, Lord. This man tests my patience." He turned his eyes back to Dagger, then switched them to Sara. "You know about this?" A hint of a smile played at Sara's lips. "Of course. You two are joined at the hip. Why should that not surprise me that you are ass deep in this homicide?" He took his time gauging each of them, wondering which one he could trust to tell the truth.

"Not sure what kind other than it was a very sophisticated bomb," Dagger said. "And before you ask, no, I didn't plant it."

"I assure you, Padre. Dagger has actually gone a week without killing anyone." The cop didn't appear amused by her comment. Sara tossed the rest of the biscuit in the bag along with the used napkins. She and Dagger had already discussed what information they would offer in the investigation. "Did you find any strange-looking weapons in there?"

Padre's attention drifted to the lake where several curious boaters were anchored off shore. "Wait. Those microwave weapons you talked about before, you think those are what we found?"

"Were they completely destroyed?"

Padre pushed the button to roll down the window, then tossed out his gum. It had lost its taste quickly, or the subject they were discussing killed his taste buds. "If you mean could any expert decipher what the hell they were and what they could be used for, no. All anyone can tell is that they were unusual. We're certainly not going to mention it in the official report."

"You should," Dagger said. He then gave the detective an abbreviated version, giving the seller's name of Mason Godfrey, but evading the true identity of the buyer, only giving a sketchy description that could define half the men in the country.

"The guy took the schematics? Shit." Padre pounded the center console. "This is bad, really bad." As he started to pull out his phone, Dagger stopped him.

"You can't tell anyone about the schematics or what the weapons were really capable of."

"Can't do that."

"You have to. Think terrorists, highest bidder and mass production. Let me handle it." Then Dagger told him that the buyer planned to sell the schematics this afternoon. "As far as the press, all they need to know is that Mason Godfrey was an arms dealer and got in bed with the wrong people. The two shooters were in the house as well as Godfrey's assistant. The press doesn't need to know the assistant's name. Just say the fourth body hasn't been identified yet and may never be. Let them think the unidentified victim had been the buyer who also died in the explosion. Mention only that there were high-tech weapons in the house that were too badly damaged to identify their true purpose. Give the story to Sheila first. She'll be forever in your debt."

Padre shook his head and mumbled, "Unfuckinbelievable. They reduce a damn microwave oven to the size of a rifle. What next? What if you don't intercept this buyer? And exactly what do you plan to do with him?"

Dagger slipped his sunglasses back on, more to hide the fury in his eyes than to shield the sun. "I haven't decided yet. Other than that, it's best that you claim plausible deniability."

49

Sara grabbed Dagger's arm. "You need to calm down before you talk to Connie."

"I'm about as calm as I'm going to get." Dagger swore as he jammed keys into each of the three dead bolts Skizzy had installed. One would have been sufficient. He tossed his keys on the desk and sat down.

"I should have known not to trust BettaTec. Bastards." Dagger placed his thumb on the imprint decal and watched the keyboard slide out and the screen appear. He tapped in the numbers then pushed the speaker button.

The android face appeared again.

"Report, please." Connie said.

"What? No hi, how are you?"

"Hi and how are you."

Dagger took a deep breath, then pulled the SIM card from his phone. "I have some pictures to upload. Just tell me how to do it."

The desk didn't have any noticeable seams or cracks, but suddenly a small section slid open with an indentation the dimensions of the SIM card. Dagger placed the card in the depression. Immediately the photos of Mason Godfrey, his assistant, and the buyer appeared. Dagger could swear he heard someone say "damn" in the background, before someone pressed a mute key.

"The buyer's name is Jonathan Keyes, and I bet you know that. After all, he is the Director of BettaTec, isn't he? I thought you said you could be trusted."

The seconds ticked on. Sara went to the bar, retrieved a can of beer and set it in front of Dagger. He popped it open and waited.

"We had our suspicions that he was involved. We had heard rumors about a deal he planned to make on his own and hoped we were wrong. You have confirmed our suspicions."

"Well, he's more dangerous than you thought. He had brought one million dollars as a good faith down payment, but when he left without the money, I suspected he planned to cover his tracks. The bomb was pretty potent. The weapons…"

"We heard the news conference. Although the weapons were destroyed, not all of the deceased have been identified."

"The Director got away. He only wanted the schematics and plans to meet with a buyer this afternoon."

"So you know where he's at?"

"I'm narrowing the location down. I'll be in touch when I have something to report." Dagger took a long swallow of beer. He didn't plan to tell them where the Director was staying nor would he admit to Connie that he had the weapons. "Is Jonathan Keyes his real name?"

"Of course not. No one is allowed to use his real name."

"Don't tell me everyone is a number."

"Only the agents are numbers. The Board members are known by one word of his or her own choosing. Mine is Connie."

"And the Director's?" Dagger finished the beer in one long swallow. He looked across the desk at Sara. She had remained unusually silent, perhaps focusing on the background sounds and voices. But Connie proved to be clever. Dagger didn't expect anything less from Connie. Dagger crumpled the can, and when Connie still hadn't replied to his question he said, "Why don't I just call him Dad?"

Several people in the background made gasping sounds. He had weighed his options whether to let Connie know he had recognized his father, then finally thought, the hell with them. It would be better to lay most of his cards on the table.

When the silence stretched, he said, "Why would you keep a man on as Director knowing he murdered his own wife and knowing he had gone rogue?" Dagger pulled a band from his pocket and pulled back his hair into a ponytail while he waited. Sara motioned to a clock on the book shelf. They needed to be at the hotel by one o'clock. He sighed heavily and was just about to power down when the reply came.

"He didn't kill me."

Dagger paused, hand raised over the power button. Sara gasped. Was this another trick by Connie and the unseen faces behind her? Had witnessing his mother's death only been another memory implanted by BettaTec?

"I don't understand," Sara said. "When we were in Nebraska Connie said she had died."

"All a ruse to give me time to assemble an alliance to counter the Director's strategies." The eyes on the android blinked.

Other than the halogram of a woman holding an infant, Dagger had no recollection of his mother. He couldn't even summon warm and fuzzy feelings. BettaTec had killed any emotion a normal man would have. Then he looked at Sara and remembered last night. Maybe they hadn't killed all of his emotions.

"You still don't trust us?"

Dagger had to laugh at that. "Sorry. Guess I've been programmed not to trust." Had it taken Connie this long to assemble like-minded accomplices? Did she have someone on the inside feeding her information? "I take it the Director has laid the groundwork for a number of other rogue projects and you aren't sure who the players are or what they involve."

"Which is why we need you. You are still our best."

"Flattery won't get you anywhere."

"It may be enough."

"You may not want me involved because the next time I see the Director, I will kill him."

"Not if you want to keep Sara safe."

"Don't…" Dagger clenched his fist and looked across the desk at his partner. Connie was playing the Sara card again. "You don't want to threaten me, Connie. I'm not very friendly when I'm threatened."

"We are well aware of that. We only have so much money in our redecorating budget."

"Humor. That's something a computer doesn't have. I do have to confess that the mother I remember isn't cruel and wouldn't threaten to harm someone to get what she wants."

"These are desperate times. Please report back soon. We believe you have a meeting to intercept."

The screen and keyboard disappeared.

50

Simon opened the door to the hotel suite. "You're sure cutting it close."

"Wow." Sara admired the high ceilings and five star décor. "You have great taste."

Simon closed the door and studied the two. "How are you doing after last night?" There was a gleam in Simon's eyes that told Dagger he was trolling for details.

"We're fine. What did this room cost me?" Dagger added quickly. A room service cart had been shoved against one wall. A staircase led to a second floor loft. Skizzy was leaning over the railing in his camo pants and tee shirt.

"Hey, can you turn the volume down? How's a guy supposed to sleep around here?"

"Thought I told you to go home?"

Skizzy stumbled his way down the steps yawning and rubbing the stubble on his face. "This is a helluva lot more comfortable."

Dagger checked his watch. Fifteen more minutes until the buyer showed up. "Give me an update."

"Just hold your horses. I need some cappo-latte-mocha stuff." Skizzy poured himself a cup of something smelling more like hazelnut than coffee.

They assembled around an octagon-shaped table. Sara preferred to stand by the window using her hawk vision to see the Director's hotel room. The drapes were opened on the wall of windows. The balcony door led to a large patio with plants, a table and two chairs. She could see the Director pacing the floor.

"The ladybug worked just fine," Skizzy reported. "We were able to track them here. Early this morning my mosquito implanted a small tracker in that assistant's neck."

"And Fredrik didn't feel the mosquito?"

"Oh yeah. He swatted at it, but the little guy got away." Skizzy dragged a box over and pointed at the contents. "Flew right back home to pappy so I can use it again."

"He has company," Sara announced.

Skizzy checked the scope and recorder, then pressed a START button. He turned the monitor toward the conference table. He and Sara took a seat and they all watched the meeting two blocks away.

"Isaac Boransky. It's a pleasure." Keyes shook hands with the former KGB agent. Boransky had a weasel thin face and eyes that revealed little, other than distrust.

Boransky motioned toward an Asian man, short and plump with glasses that appeared too large for his face. "May I present Doctor Duyong Chung."

Doctor Chung did a curt bow. The Director didn't introduce his assistant who had retreated to a corner bar. "May I offer you some coffee? Maybe something stronger?" Keyes asked.

Boransky gave a dismissive wave. "We have a plane to catch. Doctor Chung will examine the schematics then I will do the wire transfer. We trust this won't take long."

"Of course." The Director slipped out of his suit jacket, folded it carefully, and laid it across the back of the couch. Fredrik retrieved a tube from a briefcase and set it on the coffee table in front of Keyes. Keyes shook the schematics from the tube and unrolled it on the conference table. "You did see the videos I sent you?"

"Yes. Very impressive," Boransky said. "I also read the police report you sent me confirming that the prototypes were destroyed."

"Absolutely. You will have the only capability of producing these weapons." Keyes set paperweights on all four corners of the schematics to keep the blueprint from rolling back up.

"Ahhhhh." Doctor Chung's eyes widened as he leaned over the table. He pulled a small magnifier from his pocket, peeled off his glasses and studied the blueprint closer. "This is an original and there is no evidence that copies have been made," he reported.

The former KGB agent nodded toward Keyes with a self-satisfied smile. The Director's reputation had never been in doubt before. How dare he question his trustworthiness now!

Doctor Chung continued his inspection, careful not to touch the paper, his finger hovering as it followed the steps for producing the microwave weapon. He suddenly paused, looked up briefly, then swiftly scanned the remaining schematic.

"What is this?" Doctor Chung looked puzzled. "This is incomplete. It is a blueprint for a weapon but not what we are looking for. There are no instructions for dielectric heating, or how to exemplify the short millimeter waves. How do you focus the energy?" He turned to Boransky. "You have been duped."

Keyes looked from the schematics to Boransky. "I had been assured these were authentic." He tried to remain stoic. Could Johnson have had the last laugh? Could he have developed the weapons and then produced incorrect schematics? Or had Mason Godfrey deceived him and sold the true schematics before they had met?

Boransky lurched from his seat. "And the only man who knew how to build these is dead? How can we trust that the two prototypes were destroyed? Did you not think I would have these schematics verified?"

The lethal glare the Russian displayed didn't faze Keyes. He slowly rose from the table and eyed the short Asian man. "How do we know he didn't memorize the schematics and now claim they are fraudulent only so you can avoid paying the ten billion dollars?"

Boransky ripped the schematics off the table, sending the paperweights thudding to the floor. He crushed the blueprints into a ball and flung it at Keyes. "You know where you can shove those."

Keyes didn't pick up the wad of paper until his guests slammed out of the suite. Fredrik remained emotionless, hands clasped in front of him, watching the Director's hands shake in rage.

51

"Well I'll be," Simon breathed. "Either Godfrey or Johnson was one clever sonofabitch."

"I'd put my money on Johnson. After all, Godfrey had him kidnapped," Sara said. "He probably knew he wouldn't get out alive so he outmaneuvered Godfrey."

On the monitor they watched as Jonathan Keyes ripped the schematics into pieces and dropped them into a metal garbage can. Then he set the can on the balcony, lit a match, and dropped it into the can.

"I'd say his goose is cooked, yessiree." Skizzy chuckled. "Ain't nobody gonna trust him once that Russian guy starts spreadin' the news."

"You have the other weapon in a safe place, Skizzy?" Dagger opened the suitcase which contained the weapon and started to assemble it.

"Yeah, although I gotta say I don't feel safe having it around."

Dagger fastened the scope, snapped the power pack on, flipped the bipod legs down, and aimed the weapon at the hotel two blocks away. "Simon, rent a helicopter tonight and fly Skizzy over Lake Michigan. Take the damn thing apart and drop the pieces into the water, one piece every ten miles." Dagger pulled the SIM card from the recorder and unplugged the monitor.

Simon studied the assembled weapon and recognized the

look in Dagger's eyes. "What are you gonna do, Dagger?"

"You both should leave now."

Simon knew the old Dagger wouldn't have hesitated killing the Director. But Sara had given him a conscience. Leaving Dagger in Sara's hands assured his friend wouldn't do anything rash. Sara waited for the two men to gather their belongings. Skizzy quickly packed his monitor and recorder into a case, then Sara walked them to the door.

"Keep an eye on him, Sara," Simon whispered.

"I will." She closed the door after them and returned to the living room. "You do realize killing him would be too easy."

Dagger said nothing. He adjusted the scope to where Keyes looked as though he were standing on their own balcony.

"And you realize once Connie finds out how he died she will know that the weapons weren't destroyed in the explosion."

Dagger looked up and paused. He ran through scenarios in his mind and couldn't come up with one rebuttal to her comment. He still said nothing.

"Don't you need to check temperature, light source, wind, all those variables snipers use?"

"Only when using bullets," Dagger replied. He adjusted the scope again.

Two blocks away Jonathan Keyes stepped out on the spacious balcony, pulled out a chair and sat down at a wrought iron table. Fredrik appeared and set a cup of coffee and a saucer in front of the Director, then he grabbed the metal waste can with the ashes and took them inside.

Sara listened intently. "He's flushing the ashes down the toilet."

They watched Keyes, Dagger through the scope, Sara

with her hawk vision. Keyes stared off into the distance, his hands clenching and unclenching. With just one word this man could have any world figure assassinated. He could set wheels in motion that could change the course of history. Keyes' face came into full view through the scope and now Dagger could see the malice in the Director's eyes. They were dark and foreboding. The same eyes Dagger saw in the mirror every morning. He moved the weapon two inches to his right and placed his finger on the trigger. He felt Sara's hand on his shoulder. She was right. It wouldn't serve any purpose to kill him. Someone else would take his place. What would be better would be to take away his feeling of invincibility.

Sara held her breath, not sure what Dagger would do. She watched, saw his finger press the trigger, saw the beam of light stretching the two blocks. On the balcony Jonathan Keyes' ruminations were disturbed by the sound of something bubbling. At first he appeared to dismiss it, or was focused too intently on his next course of action. Then out of the corner of his eye he saw steam pouring from the cup, spilling over like dry ice in a fountain. Hearing his boss's cry of alarm, Fredrik appeared in the doorway and witnessed the cup bouncing and rattling in the saucer. They both dove for the safety of the interior, away from the window.

By the time Keyes and Fredrik hustled out of the suite and summoned a limo, Dagger and Sara had already packed up the equipment and were on the road back to Cedar Point. Connie would never know the weapons weren't destroyed. The Director could never reveal what had happened in the suite without acknowledging his part in the scheme. For now, Dagger felt one shimmer of success.

52

Dagger placed the SIM card in the depression and waited while Connie and her team watched the recording of the meeting between the Director, Doctor Chung, and Isaac Boransky. He used the bathroom in the apartment to splash water on his face and rinse out his mouth. Sara used it next while Dagger rummaged around in the refrigerator for something to eat. He pulled out two bottles of water and found a package of crackers in the cabinet. He ripped them open and offered half to Sara.

"I promise, dinner at a place of your choice as soon as we are done here." He crooked a finger under her chin and kissed her.

"Interesting transaction. We suspected Boransky's objective centered on building up the Russian military. Doctor Chung we may have to keep an eye on. We only know of his nuclear engineering breakthroughs."

Dagger returned to the desk and wondered if Connie had copied the contents of the SIM card.

"The Director is now marginalized," Connie continued. "It will be a long time until he can restore his reputation, if at all. We trust you have destroyed all evidence of this event."

As Dagger reached for the SIM card, a brief flash reduced it to ashes in less than two seconds. He had no doubt Connie had made a copy. As the monitor and keyboard started to disappear, he said aloud, "Nice job, Dagger. If I have to say so myself."

As nightfall crept on the horizon a helicopter flew low over Lake Michigan. The cool night air discouraged boaters and witnesses to the items dropped into the water.

Two patrons at The Point Restaurant on the lake shore did see the helicopter's lights. Dagger looked over at Sara whose thoughts seemed far away. He had never seen her look more beautiful. Her hair was pulled to one side and held in place with an emerald green clip.

"I know I said you could pick the restaurant, but did I have to wear a suit?"

Sara was shaken from her thoughts and forced a smile. "You're not really in a suit, just a black turtleneck and black sportcoat. And I am hungry enough to eat a whole crab leg and a side order of shrimp."

"Whatever your heart desires." He grabbed her hand and kissed it. "Now, what's bothering you?"

She watched the helicopter's lights fade in the distance and recalled how Dagger had placed the other weapon in his vault. "I think we might have made a tactical error."

Dagger waited for more.

"By boiling the contents of the Director's coffee, he now knows the weapons weren't destroyed in the explosion. He may send someone back here to search for the weapons and for the person who has them."

Dagger took a sip of his drink and tried to put himself in the Director's shoes. Yes, he would realize someone in

Cedar Point still had the weapons. "True," Dagger conceded. "On the other hand, he could also assume that person got out of town as soon as he could, to stay on the move, maybe even tail him. And don't forget, Skizzy placed that tracker on Fredrik. He and the Director are headed to Canada. We can keep tabs on him."

Sara nodded. It made sense. "Either way," she said, "we'll be ready."

"Yes, we will."

"Aren't you the lovely one." An elderly woman in a colorful costume held a basket of fresh flowers. Her accent had a Scottish or Irish lilt to it, and she had tucked her gray hair under a floral hat. "Compliments of the house, my dear." The woman set a bouquet of flowers on the table next to Sara.

"Thank you." Sara smiled as the woman wandered to the next table. "That was so sweet of her."

The waitress brought their drinks, took their order, and gathered up the menus. Dagger raised his glass. "Love is composed of a single soul occupying two bodies."

"Aristotle. I'm impressed." Sara tapped her glass against his.

They enjoyed a leisurely dinner and an after dinner drink. An hour later as they gathered their things to head home, Sara saw something drop from the bouquet of flowers. Dagger picked up what looked like an envelope. He opened it and pulled out a card with the picture of a betta fish on the front.

"How did that...?" Sara knew they wouldn't be able to find the flower lady. Dagger turned the card over. It read:

"Nice job, six-one-seven."

At three in the morning, Sara stirred. A sound had awakened her, a clicking or soft beep. She rose up on one elbow and listened. She stripped out the normal night sounds—the hum from the cable box, the clicking from the ice cube maker, tapping of leaves falling on the skylights in the living room, and the shuffling of the night creatures outside. Had the sound come from outside or inside of the house? She had thought inside, but whatever she had heard, it had stopped.

Dagger opened his eyes. "What's wrong, babe?"

"Shhhh. Thought I heard something." Sara gave it several more seconds, then laid back down and rolled close to Dagger, felt his arms wrap tightly around her. "Guess it was nothing." Still, she couldn't shake the feeling of uneasiness.

In Dagger's vault the screen above the desk had turned on, alerting him to a change. One of the pulsing red lights indicating the location of BettaTec's satellites had moved. Although one continued its route in the lower hemisphere, the one in the upper hemisphere had moved to a trajectory which sent it over Cedar Point, Indiana.

CPSIA information can be obtained at www.ICGtesting.com
Printed in the USA
LVOW050518040313

322496LV00001B/3/P